A PLACE OF PEACE

When Nell participates in a transatlantic house-swap, going to stay in New England on the beautiful Barratt Island for three months, she hopes to escape the shame she left behind in Derbyshire. She soon meets gorgeous police chief Colm Barratt — and scheming socialite Julia Silkwood, whose husband's health seems to be failing suspiciously quickly. With Nell's overactive imagination running riot, and her past about to catch up with her, she fears she could lose Colm forever.

SALLY QUILFORD

A PLACE OF PEACE

Complete and Unabridged

LINFORD
Leicester

First published in Great Britain in 2014

First Linford Edition
published 2015

A catalogue record for this book is available
from the British Library.

ISBN 978–1–4448–2588–6

Published by
F. A. Thorpe (Publishing)
Anstey, Leicestershire

Set by Words & Graphics Ltd.
Anstey, Leicestershire
Printed and bound in Great Britain by
T. J. International Ltd., Padstow, Cornwall

This book is printed on acid-free paper

1

'The house is called *Canopache*. It's a Native American word meaning 'A place of peace',' Colm Barratt explained as he showed Nell Palmer around the house, situated on Barratt Island just off the New England mainland. Nell hoped it would be a place of peace for her, after all the upheaval of the past couple of years.

She could hardly take the house in. What was she going to do with all that space?

It stood in a row of other similar houses, all built from the pale clapboard that characterised the islands of New England. Canopache had four bedrooms and three bathrooms, and a kitchen into which Nell could put her whole present house. From the windows she could see the bay. The deck outside covered one hundred and eighty degrees, with the beach and the ocean on all sides.

The open-plan house was big and beautiful, and Nell could have said much the same about her tour guide. Colm Barratt must have been at least six feet four inches tall, with broad shoulders tapering to narrow hips. He was about forty-two years old, with blue eyes, dark hair which was slightly greying at the temples, and an honest, handsome face. When he smiled, his grin was lopsided, giving him a boyish look. But his dark uniform, that of the chief of police, also gave him an authority with which no one would argue. Nell feared for any bad guys who tried to take on Colm Barratt.

'I think your sister is going to be really disappointed with my two-up two-down railway cottage,' Nell said. 'I had no idea her home would be so big.'

'We build everything bigger in America,' Barrett said, flashing that boyish grin.

'You certainly do,' she murmured. 'I

mean, the house. The house is big. All the houses are. They make British houses look like rabbit hutches.'

'I'm sure Patty will love your place,' Colm said, as if understanding her embarrassment. 'She always wanted to visit Europe; then her daughter, Celine, decided to marry an Englishman, and this house-swap thing on the Internet was a godsend to her.'

'You're not going to the wedding?'

'I already attended their civil wedding in New York. The British wedding is for the groom's family, but Patty still wanted to go as mother of the bride. My brothers are going, so the Barratt family are well-represented. She says you're not far from where Mary Queen of Scots was kept prisoner.'

'That's right. Chatsworth House in Derbyshire. She'll be able to see the bedroom where Mary slept. Patty said your family came over with the Pilgrim Fathers.'

Colm laughed. It was a low, sexy sound. 'You ask anyone around here and they all did. The Mayflower must have been some big boat, like the TARDIS the Doctor flies around in. But we're of Irish descent, and I don't think the Pilgrim Fathers had much time for Catholics.'

Nell laughed. 'No, perhaps not. Thanks for showing me around, Mr Barratt.'

'Please, call me Colm. May I call you Ellen?'

'It's Nell, actually.'

He led her back into the kitchen. It had a row of Shaker-style cabinets on one side, then a huge cooking and preparation island, with a dining-cum-living area looking out through a pair of French doors. Nell decided straight away that this was where she was going to spend most of her time.

'I got you a few groceries in,' Colm explained. 'I wasn't sure what you liked, but there's pasta, sauce, cheese; and I remembered you probably drank tea, being English, so I called in to a store on the mainland that sells English food,

4

and got you some Yorkshire Tea. Is that right?'

'That's perfect, thank you. What do I owe you?'

'Nothing. Patty already told me on the phone last night that you'd done the same for her when she arrived in England. She also said to tell you that she'd never tried a Chocolate Hobnob before, but now she has, she will never go back. Whatever that means. Will Mr Palmer be joining you?'

'There isn't a Mr Palmer. Except my dad. I was married, but Palmer is my maiden name.'

'Ah . . . I'm sorry . . .'

'Oh, don't look so worried. He's alive, but living with a thirty-year-old nurse. Oh dear, I hadn't meant to sound that bitter. Sorry. I'm fine with it. Honestly. They say life begins at forty; well, he broke up with me on my thirty-fifth birthday, and I've been determined that I won't let that be the end.'

'You're thirty-five? You don't look it.'

'Thank you. But I'm thirty-six now.'

Something shone in Colm's eyes and she wondered if he was pleased to find out she was older than he had thought. *There you go, imagining things again*, Nell chided herself. *That's what got you into this trouble in the first place. Too many nights spent alone . . .* She mentally shook herself. Anyway, she had come away to write her book, not to indulge in a holiday romance.

'Thank you again, Mr . . . Barratt. I mean, Colm. I'm sure I'll have everything I need.'

'Right, well, I'll leave you. I've written my cell number next to all the phones, so if you have any problems, you just give me a call. Any time, day or night.'

'I'm sure your wife would love that.'

'My wife, Mary, died six years ago.'

'I'm so sorry.'

'Thank you.' He nodded his head in acknowledgement of her sympathy.

'Do you have any children, Colm?'

'I do indeed. I have a daughter,

Kathleen, and a two-year-old granddaughter, Bonnie. They live on the mainland. It's hard for the young here to buy homes. The holidaymakers hike up the prices.'

'Tell me about it,' said Nell with feeling. 'The village I live in is the same. Weekenders have forced prices up so that the young have to leave. I'm lucky in that my house was a real fixer-upper. In fact, it still is . . . ' Nell imagined Patty's disappointment.

'Patty will love it, I promise you. Now, I really have to get back to the station.'

'Oh, of course. I haven't offered you a drink though . . . '

'Don't worry. You get settled in, and I'll maybe call in for coffee during the week to see how you are.'

'I'd like that.' And Nell realised that she was telling the truth. Holiday romance or not, she liked having Colm Barratt around. He made her feel safe.

★ ★ ★

Julia Silkwood watched through her kitchen window as Colm Barratt got into his patrol car and left Canopache.

'It's a woman,' she said to her husband, Merle. He sat at the kitchen counter, trying to open a box of chocolates. Wrapping paper and a card littered the otherwise spotless surface. 'Good-looking, too. Not that Colm will be interested. His heart still belongs to Mary. I do think it's about time he married again. Oh, what are you doing, Merle? You really shouldn't be eating those. They're not good for you.'

Julia stalked across the kitchen and took the chocolate box from her husband, tearing it open and spilling chocolates everywhere. 'Now look what you've done.'

'I didn't do it.'

'No, that's right. Blame me for everything.'

'I'm not blaming you, Julia. The seal was stuck.'

'No, it wasn't. You're just weak.'

'I'm just getting over gastric flu.'

'Man-flu, you mean!' Julia sighed, assuming a martyred look. 'It doesn't matter.'

She went to the cupboard under the sink and took out some cleaning cloths and a spray bottle. Caring little if any of the spray went onto Merle's chocolates, she attacked the counter with vigour, sweeping up the wrappings and throwing them in the bin, and then cleaning the surface to within an inch of its life. 'It's always me who has to clean up. Mary always said that Colm was really good around the house.'

'Yeah, you could have been married to him.'

'Yes, I could have, now you come to mention it. He had his eye on me once, when he was on the football team in high school. But Mary had all that Irish red hair, and who can compete with that? I had to settle for you . . . eventually.'

'I'm sorry I've been such a disappointment.'

'Life is a disappointment,' said Julia,

throwing the cleaning stuff back under the kitchen sink. 'But we have to make the best of it, don't we? I suppose I shall have to make friends with her, or she'll think I'm a snob.'

'With who?'

'The Britisher who's staying in Patty's house, that's who. Now, I wonder if she likes apple pie? No, no, they eat that strange stuff over there, don't they? Spotted Dick.'

Merle started to laugh, but stopped very quickly when Julia shot him a stern look. He popped a chocolate into his mouth and left her alone to stare out across the street at Canopache.

* * *

Nell wandered around the house alone and with the air of a woman who could not quite believe her luck. For three whole months this house would be hers. She tried not to think of being back at work in the library in the winter months, and of all those interminable

10

evenings when it grew dark at three-thirty in the afternoon.

She would complete the book that she had always promised herself she would write, and then maybe she would get an agent. Unpacking, she took the partial manuscript from her suitcase: *The Life and Times of Michel de Montaigne*. Nell had found out lots about Montaigne and his rather dubious relationship with his niece. That would get the publishers salivating. It was a pity she could not read Middle French, but that did not matter. She had read all his essays and felt she knew the man well. It was also a pity that, less than one chapter in, she had stalled, finding that her handling of the subject was a bit dull and uninteresting.

But that was because she had not had time to get into it. First came the divorce, and then all that stuff with Mr Kemp next door . . . She sighed fitfully, wondering what Colm Barratt would think if he knew the truth about her.

There was no reason he should, and

she would certainly not make that mistake again. 'You spend too much time reading books,' her mother had always told her. For Nell's parents, reading was a wasted pastime, and akin to laziness. Yet all they ever did was sit in front of the television, watching old episodes of *Inspector Morse* or *Only Fools and Horses*, or go down to the local working men's club to play bingo.

'She's got ideas above her station,' her father had said when Nell announced she wanted to train to be a librarian. 'What's wrong with a shop, like our Sandra?' Sandra was Nell's elder sister by fifteen years, and always Mum and Dad's clear favourite because she was happy to stay where she was in life. Sometimes Nell envied her sister's acceptance of everything. Sandra was one of the happiest people Nell knew.

Despite their parents showing favouritism to the elder sister, the girls got on very well, and it was Sandra who had found Nell the house-swap website when she needed to escape. 'It'll all die down, pet,' Sandra had said, kissing Nell goodbye at East Midlands Airport. 'Something else will happen and people will forget.'

'I hope so. I feel such an idiot. I reckon it was Mum and Dad's fault, making us watch all those crime shows when we were kids. If they'd just let me read instead . . . '

Sandra laughed. 'So it wasn't all those Agatha Christies you read your way through when you were sixteen, then?'

'*Touché*,' said Nell, grinning. 'At least I wasn't reading out the dirty bits in *Princess Daisy* under the bedclothes.'

'Only because *I* read them out to *you*. Now, promise me you'll be okay. I love you, you know.'

Nell smiled, remembering the huge hug Sandra had given her. She wished her sister could be with her — but, with a grandchild due in the summer, Sandra would not leave her daughter behind.

Nell felt a pang of regret. Maybe having children would have helped her to be more grounded. It would be hard to spy on one's neighbours if you always had to be on the lookout for your children drinking bleach or eating worms.

Throwing her manuscript aside, promising to get to it when she was not so jetlagged, Nell went to the window. The bedroom, which looked like something out of a Martha Stewart catalogue, was on the corner of the house, with a curved wrap-around window giving a grand vista of the ocean. Yes, she would definitely be inspired here.

As she gazed out, not wanting the view to end, she saw a woman walking from the house across the road, carrying something on a plate. A man followed her. Nell had the crazy image that the woman had the man on a lead, but she realised that he only looked like a puppy dog, dragging along behind.

She realised, with some horror, that

they were headed for Canopache. She fixed a smile on her face. She had been warned that in America people often arrived with cakes and other produce; and whilst she would have hated anyone to do that in Britain, she knew she had to fit in on the island.

She had reached the front door before the woman rang the bell. 'Hello,' she said, smiling.

'Oh, hello. I'm Julia Silkwood and I've brought you some chocolate cake.' Julia was a tall, slender woman, with high cheekbones and the stiffly-coiffured hair favoured by First Ladies.

'Well . . . thank you.'

'I was going to make Spotted Dick, but I didn't have any suet in the house.'

'Oh, well, I'm sure the cake will be lovely. And you are . . . ?' She turned to the man.

'Don't mind him. That's Merle. My husband.'

'Oh, well, thank you Julia *and Merle*.'

The man smiled shyly and with warmth, but the woman had an icy brittleness about her, and an almost rictus-like grin. Like a Stepford Wife.

Julia and Merle waited, and Nell realised that she was expected to invite them in. 'I, er . . . I'm still unpacking,' she said, realising she was being very ungracious, but too tired to deal with neighbours. 'But maybe you'd like to come over for coffee when I get settled in properly.'

'Of course, you have much to do,' said Julia, but in tones that said she did not understand at all.

'But . . . oh, it doesn't matter,' Nell said, with more grace. 'I'll have long enough to unpack and the cake is very welcome. Why don't you come in for coffee and we'll all enjoy a slice?'

'That's fine, ma'am,' said Merle, earning a frozen look from his wife. 'You don't want us intruding. You get your unpacking finished. Like you say, there's plenty of time.'

'Well, it looks like that's settled,' said Julia.

'I really am grateful for the cake,' said

Nell, as they wandered back across the road to their own house. Merle turned and gave her a friendly wave, but Julia kept her head rigidly staring ahead. In that moment, Nell decided she liked Merle but detested Julia.

She took the cake to the kitchen and, taking a fork from the drawer, scooped out a piece and ate it. It had a strangely bitter aftertaste. 'So this is what guilt tastes like,' she said, kicking herself for behaving so ungratefully. She put the cake into the freezer, and made herself a decent meal with the food that Colm had provided.

When she was violently sick later that night, she put it down to Julia's cake rather than Colm's supplies.

2

By the time she awoke the next morning to the sound of waves crashing against the beach, Nell had pushed aside all thoughts of Julia's cooking poisoning her. It had merely been a reaction to a woman whom she did not like. And that was hardly Julia's fault. Nell had not really given the poor woman a chance, terrified as she was by the way Americans immediately made friends with people.

In Britain, it often took months before new neighbours spoke to each other. Sometimes it was years. In fact, she had lived in her house ten years before speaking to Mr Kemp, and then only because . . . She pushed it to the back of her mind. She was supposed to be forgetting all that.

If Julia Silkwood had been icy, then it was because Nell had not exactly been welcoming. She vowed to put that right as soon as she had eaten breakfast.

With the dishes popped into the dishwasher, Nell went across the road and knocked on the door. She fought off the feeling that she had been watched the whole time. There was only one other house on that road, and it was some five hundred yards away.

'Good morning,' said Julia when she answered the door. There was a question in her voice.

'Good morning, Julia. I just wanted to say thank you so much for the chocolate cake. It was delicious. And I'm sorry if I seemed a little unwelcoming last night. I was jetlagged.'

That much had been true, and was probably the real reason that Nell had been sick.

'You did have a long trip,' said Julia, nodding. Suddenly she smiled and her whole demeanour changed. 'I should have thought before bothering you.'

'No, of course not. It was very kind of you. Anyway, I wondered, since you live on the island, whether you knew where to go around here for some decent food. Not that the cake wasn't very decent. It was yummy. I mean, you know, restaurants and suchlike.'

'Suchlike? Oh, I love your accent,' said Julia, with a warmth that Nell had been sure the woman lacked. She had obviously been wrong about her. 'Of course, I'll show you around the island. Let me get my car keys.'

'Oh, there's no need to put yourself out. Just point me in the right direction.'

'It's no trouble. Merle is in bed, feeling unwell. He hasn't been right since that accident at work.'

The accident, Julia explained as they drove towards the main town, had come about as a result of some machinery becoming faulty. 'Then again, if it hadn't, we wouldn't be living on this wonderful island. They paid him a lot of money to go away. But poor Merle's hands have never been the same since. It crushed all his fingers. I do what I can for him, but . . . '

'It must be difficult,' said Nell.

'I survive,' said Julia.

'Well, yes, but I meant for him too.'

'Oh he's alright, getting waited on all the time. And under my feet!' Julia laughed, and for a moment Nell did not like her much again. She really had to get over her irrational dislike of a woman who had shown her nothing but kindness.

'I love the houses here,' Nell said, getting onto safer ground. 'They have a colonial look about them.'

'They're called Cape Cod style,' said Julia, 'They were originally built in the seventeenth century, and some on the island are that old, with others from the Civil War. That's the smaller houses. But nowadays each family builds according to their needs, so they can get much bigger.'

'Like that one up there,' said Nell, pointing to a house high up on the cliffs. It was in the colonial style of white clapboard, with a deck around

21

the bottom and a balcony on the top storey.

'That's Colm Barratt's house,' Julia said. 'Of course, he was devoted to his dear late wife.'

'Yes, I got that impression.'

'Mary was very beautiful. Colm won't settle for anything less than perfection.' Julia cast a sideways glance at Nell which was none too complimentary, and then concentrated on the road again. 'So I can't see him ever marrying again even if he is the most eligible bachelor on the island.'

'You won't catch me marrying again either,' Nell agreed, shaking off the feeling she was being warned.

'Oh. So you're divorced?'

'That's right.'

'What happened?'

'A thirty-year-old nurse.' There was much more to it than that, but Nell found the shorthand version was understood more easily than the real saga of her relationship with Rick.

'Ah, men are pigs when all is said and

done. You can do better.'

Maybe Nell would like Julia Silkwood after all.

'Have you lived on the island all your life?' Nell asked, as they drank coffee and ate cake in a little diner overlooking the harbour. Fishing boats and pleasure cruisers sailed in and out, and Nell thought she might quite like to hire a boat and sail around the island. A few tourists wandered along the promenade, idling the day away. 'It's so idyllic.'

'I was born here, and went to school here,' Julia replied. 'But then I had to leave for the mainland, to get a job. There's not much to be doing, except in the summer months when the tourists come over.'

'Is that where you met Merle? On the mainland?'

'No. We went to school together, but he's my second husband. My first husband died.'

'Oh, I'm so sorry to hear that.'

'It took a long time to get over it.'

'And then you met Merle. It must have been nice, finding an old friend when you needed it.'

'Yes, I suppose it was. Only things never turn out quite as you expect them to.'

'Oh.' Nell did not know what to say to that. She did not know Julia enough to pry too hard into her marriage. 'But you're back on the island. That must make you happy.'

'Oh yes. That was a dream come true. Before Merle's settlement we could not have afforded it. This is where I belong.'

'I know what you mean. I was lucky enough to be able to buy a property in my village before weekenders pushed the prices up. I loved living there.'

'Loved?' Julia had clearly picked up on the past tense.

'Oh . . . I mean, love. I love it there.' Nell thought if she could say it often enough it would be true. And it was, to a certain extent. Only she had made a complete fool of herself, and now she did not know if she could face her neighbours again. 'But it will be nice to have three months' break. You know what they say about a change being as good as a rest. And Patty's house is truly lovely.'

'Yes, it is.'

The diner door opened, and Nell turned to see Colm enter. He took off his police cap. 'Good morning ladies,' he said, with that sexy lopsided grin.

'Good morning, Colm,' said Julia.

'Good morning,' Nell said, feeling a little shy in his presence. He made the diner look tiny. A few more of the punters, whom Nell presumed were island natives, bid him hello. 'Julia has very kindly been showing me around,' she explained.

'You couldn't ask for a better tour guide.'

'Why don't you join us, Colm?' asked Julia, moving along the bench on her side. Her face assumed its usual frozen expression when he sat next to Nell instead.

Without being asked, the waitress came along with a cup of coffee and a slice of Key lime pie for Colm. He thanked her and she went away preening. The man certainly knew how to charm the ladies!

'How are you settling in?' he asked, turning to Nell.

'Very well, thank you. I was just saying how wonderful the house is. I hardly know what to do with all that room.'

'Patty's always saying the same, since her children moved out,' Colm said.

'Do you think she might sell?' asked Julia. 'We're looking for somewhere bigger.'

'I . . . I don't know.' Colm looked a little taken aback. 'I think she's happy there.'

'Well, she can't be if she's gone off to Europe for three months. If I had a home like Patty's, I'd never want to leave it.'

'Still haven't found that perfect spot, eh, Julia?' Colm laughed. 'How many homes is that now? It's got to be at least one every two years since we left school. I tell you, Nell, this lady has had more housewarming parties than I've had birthdays.'

'Well, we weren't all born into money, or had a father who left a fortune to his children, Colm,' Julia said, blushing and looking a little bit peeved. 'If I had a house like yours up on the cliffs, I'd be happy to stay there. But some of us have to rise up the property ladder.'

'Of course, Julia,' said Colm, abashed. 'I didn't mean to cause offence.'

'This is lovely, isn't it?' Nell twittered, fearing that she had bumbled into something sensitive. 'Sitting in a coffee shop with that wonderful view. I'd be quite happy to live in a shack on this island.'

'I have one at the end of my garden,' said Colm. 'Feel free to move in come September.'

'Careful,' said Nell. 'I may take you up on that.'

'I'd be delighted if you did.'

'Well . . . ' Julia slammed her coffee cup down. 'I really ought to get back to Merle. I should never have left him as it is.'

'Oh, I'm sorry, Julia.' Nell winced inwardly, and felt her cheeks flaming. 'I shouldn't have bothered you.'

'I'm sure Merle will be fine,' said Colm quietly. 'Never let it be said that we don't have time for neighbours, hey, Julia?'

'Of course, you're right, Colm,' Julia said, chastened. 'I'll go and pay the bill.'

'No, let me,' Nell protested.

'Don't even think of it. As Colm says, we always have time for neighbours.'

Whilst Julia was at the counter, paying, Nell muttered to Colm, 'Is she alright? I mean . . . I just feel like I keep saying the wrong thing. Then she's fine again, and . . . '

'She's a good woman,' said Colm, and for a moment Nell thought she was being rebuked. 'But she can be a bit changeable. She's had a tough life.'

'Losing her first husband must have been difficult.'

'Yeah . . . ' Colm's eyes clouded over, and he seemed to be about to say something else, but decided against it. 'You need to meet more people here.'

'What plot are you two hatching?' said Julia when she returned. She might have been joking, but Nell was not so sure.

'I'm thinking, maybe I'll hold a barbecue and introduce Nell to more of the neighbours,' said Colm. 'I hope you're not a vegetarian, Nell, because I grill the best rib eye steaks this side of Texas.'

Nell laughed. 'No, I'm not vegetarian, but I don't want to put you to any trouble.'

'It's no trouble. Patty told me I had to take care of you, and I don't want to incur the wrath of my sister. She's got a wicked temper.'

'She's as gentle as a lamb,' said Julia.

'Oh, to you, maybe,' Colm laughed.

'But to her three little brothers, she's a tyrant.'

Nell giggled. 'I can't imagine you being anyone's little brother.'

'Been bossed around by an elder sister all my life,' said Colm with a twinkle in his eyes. 'But I don't mind. In my experience, women usually do know best.'

'I'll remember that if I ever marry you,' said Julia. Nell knew then that Julia was not joking.

Julia was in love with Colm, Nell thought, and had been for a long time. That was probably why she was unhappy with Merle. Poor Merle. Nell empathised with him. He was a nice, gentle man, but weedy-looking. There was no way he could compete with a man as strong and virile as Colm.

Nell definitely had bumbled into something, but at the time she was not sure what.

★ ★ ★

Two weeks later, Colm took some steaks out of the freezer, smiling to himself. He had wanted an excuse to see more of Nell, and Julia had helped with that.

He had known Julia since they were at school, and understood that she could be difficult to be around. He did not want Nell to go home with the idea that all the islanders were capable of blowing hot and cold in equal measure.

And, if he were honest, he liked looking at Nell. He liked the warmth in her gentle grey eyes, and the way her sleek blonde hair curved into a bob around her pretty chin. He liked the way she talked, and the way she laughed. She looked younger than her true age, and he had been relieved to learn she was in her thirties. If she had been in her twenties, as he first believed, then he would have feared she was too young for him.

Maybe after the barbecue tonight he would ask her out for dinner alone. The thought made him smile. It had been a long time since he had dated, but maybe it was time. His daughter Kathleen was always telling him to 'get back out there'. He looked at the picture of Mary that he had clipped to the fridge. It had been taken on their boat, during one their last day-trips before she died. With a scarf tied around her head to hide the effects of the chemotherapy, she looked tired but happy. 'Do you think it will be okay if I ask her out, sweetheart?' he asked. She smiled back at him encouragingly, and he took it as a sign of her blessing.

Just as he was leaving the house to go to the station, the telephone rang. 'Oh, Colm, thank goodness I caught you.'

'Patty? Is that you, honey?'

'Yes, it's late here, but I wanted to catch you before you went to work.'

'What's happened? Are you okay?'

'Oh yes, I'm fine, Colm. Don't worry about me.'

'Is Nell's house okay?'

'Yes, it's absolutely charming, and in the prettiest little village, but . . . '

'What? Have you had enough of Europe already?'

'No, listen Colm. I got talking to the neighbours. That took some doing. They're a bit reserved here in England, but they soon warmed up when they realised where I was staying. Colm, you won't believe what I heard about Nell.' Patty laughed, but it was an awkward sound, like she was not sure if what she was about to say was amusing or not.'

'What?'

'Well, she got it into her head that her neighbour, a perfectly charming gentleman called Mr Kemp, had committed a murder. She got the police involved and everything, saying that one night she'd seen Mr Kemp in the bedroom window strangling his wife.'

'So she did the right thing to call the police . . . ' said Colm, knowing there was more to come.'

'But that's just it. The wife was missing for a while and there was a bit of a search for her, but she turned up quite happily at her sister's house in

Blackpool. She and Mr Kemp had argued and she'd left home, but she most certainly was not dead.'

'So it was a misunderstanding?'

'Colm, Nell Palmer is as nutty as a bag of peanuts, honey. Everyone here says so. It even made the papers, and her own mother says she lives in a dream world. No wonder she had to get out of England. I'm going to find an excuse to return early, but I can't come back until after Celine's wedding in a fortnight. I can't let her down, Colm. But as soon as I can get back home I will. I'll pay Nell Palmer's plane fare back myself if I have to. Just keep an eye on her until I can get back. She's mad. Totally mad.'

3

Nell was beginning to think that Julia Silkwood was not the only one who blew hot and cold. She had been at the barbecue for half an hour and Colm had barely spoken to her, except to say hello and offer her a drink. He had not been as icy as Julia, but there was a reserved look behind his eyes she could not mistake.

Groups of people stood around chatting, whilst fairy lights twinkled in the trees. A gentle breeze blew up from the ocean, wafting the aroma of steak and onions in the night air.

'How are you enjoying the island?' a woman asked Nell. She struggled to remember the woman's name. Wendy, that was it. She was a pretty and curvaceous woman who clearly enjoyed every bit of the food on offer.

'I love it here, Wendy,' she said. That

much was true. 'The last couple of weeks have been heavenly, exploring the island or just sitting on the beach, watching the ocean and the fishing boats.' She had not got much writing done, but decided that she would call her wasted time 'research'. Not that Michel de Montaigne had ever set foot in New England. Still, the Old World atmosphere must be of some help in her creative endeavours. 'I keep expecting people to burst into song. You know, about some lady called June busting out all over.'

'Oh, I love *Carousel*.'

'Yes, me too.'

'I played Julie in the school play,' said Wendy. 'Years ago now. I didn't really have the voice for it, but we weren't exactly Glee stars in those days, and nor were we expected to be. We didn't have auto-tuning either!'

Nell smiled. 'I remember my own warbled attempts as Nancy in the school production of *Oliver!*. Were you at school with Colm and Julia?'

'Yes I was, though a couple of years below them. In fact, Colm's wife Mary was one of my best friends.'

'Ah. I've heard nothing but good about her.'

'And nor will you.'

'Julia seems to think that Colm will never marry again.'

'Oh, I think men always do,' said Wendy. 'They need us women around. It's women who tend to stay widows. Apart from Julia.' For a moment the warmth left Wendy's face.

'She said she'd lost her first husband.'

'Hmm.'

Nell searched Wendy's face for more. There was definitely a story there she was not being told. She pushed the thought away. She had no need to indulge in fantasies nowadays. Staying on the island was living the dream.

'Colm, we're dying of thirst here,' said Wendy, playfully. 'Some host you are.'

'Forgive me,' said Colm, who was

just coming from the kitchen with a tub of coleslaw. 'What can I get you ladies?'

'Have you ever tried Long Island Iced Tea, Nell?' Wendy asked.

'No, but I've heard of it.'

'Then that's what we'll have. Let's show Nell a real taste of America. They used to drink it during Prohibition, you know, Nell, because it resembled tea.'

'That's bunkum,' Colm called over his shoulder as he went back to the house, having deposited the coleslaw on a long table near to the grill. 'It wasn't invented till the seventies.' A few minutes later he returned with the cocktail that included a mix of vodka, gin, tequila and rum, with a splash of cola.

'Hmm, delicious,' said Nell, realising she would have to drink it very carefully or she might end up making a fool of herself. 'Have you heard from your sister?' she asked Colm, who at least seemed to have stuck around. His eyes clouded over. 'Oh dear, is the house not to her liking?'

'She says the house is charming,' said Colm. 'Really charming. The village is too.'

He was holding something back, Nell was sure of it, but she felt shy about cross-examining him at his own barbecue. 'Thank you for doing this,' she said, shyly. 'Everyone has been so kind.'

'You're welcome.'

'Where is Merle tonight?' Nell asked Colm. Julia had arrived ten minutes earlier, but alone. She had not yet spoken to Nell. In fact, she had not spoken to Nell for several days, and whenever Nell thought of going to pay a visit, Julia jumped into her car and drove off somewhere for hours at a time.

'Julia says he's unwell.'

'He hasn't been the same since his accident,' said Wendy. Then, under her breath: 'Or his marriage.'

'Now, Wendy . . . ' Colm's voice held a warning note.

'Oh, go away, Colm and let us women gossip. You men are rubbish at it.' She winked at Nell.

'I'll get back to my barbecue then,' said Colm, his eyes full of laughter. It was the most relaxed he had seemed all night.

'Thank you again for doing this,' Nell said to him. 'It's great to meet everyone else.'

'I'm glad you're enjoying it,' said Colm. He seemed to come to a decision. 'Maybe we could talk later, when I've finished my hosting duties.'

'I'd like that.'

Wendy drew Nell away to a long fence that overlooked the sea. 'I haven't seen Colm smile like that for a long time,' she said. 'You've brought a twinkle to his eyes.'

'I hardly think it's me.'

'Oh, don't be so modest. You're pretty and charming and just right for him. He's been on his own too long.'

'That's very kind of you to say. Now — ' She lowered her voice. ' — what were you going to tell me about Julia?'

'Oh now, there's a story, but ... ' Wendy stopped, looking up towards the main garden. 'Oh, it looks like Merle has decided to come after all.'

Sure enough, Merle Silkwood was just coming around the side of the house, carrying a six-pack of beer.

'He doesn't look well,' said Nell. His face was ashen. She moved away from Wendy, wanting to give the man a welcome, because everyone else just seemed to be looking from him to Julia then back again. 'Hello, Merle, how are you feeling?'

'I'm fine, thanks, Nell. Nothing that one of Colm's steaks won't fix.'

'They're certainly as delicious as they smell.'

'You should be in bed,' said a familiar icy voice behind them.

'Now, Julia, don't start.' Merle looked like a schoolboy who had been found with his hands in the cookie jar. 'I told you I was well enough to come. You said I should stay home. But I got friends here too, and I never see 'em anymore.'

41

'It is good to see you, Merle,' said Wendy. 'Come on, let's find you one of those steaks.'

Nell could only describe the rest of the evening as 'strained'. Julia hardly spoke to anyone, sitting alone in a corner. Nell attempted to start up a conversation with her, on account of Julia being the second person who had befriended her when she came to the island, but the lady made it plain she was not interested in anything Nell had to say.

'Nell,' said Colm, when a few people had left. Only Wendy and her husband Ted, and Julia and Merle, remained. Merle and Julia seemed to be hanging around, almost challenging each other to be the first to leave.

'Yes, Colm?'

'Could you help me carry these things back into the house?'

'Of course.'

Wendy stood back, with a secret smile on her face, and stopped her husband Ted from helping. She muttered something to him and then he smiled too.

Nell followed Colm into the kitchen, carrying the leftover coleslaw and a plate full of sweetcorn husks. 'Where do these go?' she asked.

'Oh, right over here in the waste disposal,' said Colm 'Actually, I wanted to get you alone to ask if you'd like to go out for dinner one night.'

'Yes, I'd love to.'

'Great . . . '

'You seem a bit doubtful. Has . . . has Patty said anything?' Nell decided then that he must know why she had left England, but she was in the awkward position of not wanting to bring it up, just in case he had not actually heard anything.

'Gossip is a terrible thing,' said Colm. 'Despite what Wendy said. It can ruin nice people.'

'Yes, yes it can.' Now, was he talking about her personally? Or was he alluding to the gossip about Julia?

'I prefer to judge people as they behave toward me.'

'So do I,' said Nell.

'Good. I'm glad that's understood. So, how about I take you out tomorrow night? There's a great seafood restaurant over on the mainland. We could go over on my boat.'

'I'd love that.' Nell nodded enthusiastically. Why have wild fantasies when the dream was standing there in front of you? She was realistic enough to know that whatever was happening between her and Colm would not last, but it did not matter. She would just enjoy it for what it was.

They went back outside, both having gone quiet, but it was a comfortable silence, full of the anticipation of the evening to come.

'Best steak ever,' Merle said, finishing off a plateful of steak, mushrooms and onions. 'All a dying man could wish for.'

'You dying, Merle?' asked Colm, his handsome face becoming serious for a moment.

'Well, you know, it feels like that some days,' said Merle. 'Since the accident.'

'Don't be so dramatic,' said Julia. 'We should be going. Nell, we'll give you a lift.'

Nell could not have argued even if she'd wanted to. She found herself bundled towards Julia's car, and having to endure the thunderous silence between Julia and Merle. When they reached Canopache, she wished them both goodnight and hurried into the house. She looked back to see Merle's wan gaze following her up the garden path. She smiled encouragement at him, little realising then that it was the last time she would see him alive.

4

It was still light when Nell and Colm left the island for the mainland, but the sun was beginning to set. The waves lapped gently at the side of the boat. Nell sat at the front, looking out, revelling in the gentle breeze on her face. She had dressed in a white maxi dress with a crocheted bolero top and a pair of gladiator sandals, hoping it was suitable attire for an evening of sailing.

Colm, stood at the wheel, looked every bit the captain in a white polo shirt and white jeans, with a peaked cap set on his head at an angle. It was fair to say she had never seen such a handsome man in her life, and probably never would again. The idea made her melancholy, but she was determined to fight it and enjoy his company while it lasted.

'What are you thinking?' Colm asked.

'I'm thinking this is the loveliest way to spend an evening,' she said, getting up and walking back to him. She took the seat next to him.

'I agree. We've got great weather for it too.'

'Do you get very bad weather here?'

'Sure. In the winter we can be totally cut off from the mainland. There's a storm coming in soon. If you'd lived here long enough, you'd feel it in the air. And don't forget, it wasn't far from here that the *Titanic* sank.'

'That's very comforting.' Nell laughed.

'Don't worry. We won't be going near any icebergs tonight. I've told my brother to keep them all up his end.'

'Your brother? Oh yes, you have two brothers, don't you? What do they do?'

'Kian, my middle brother, works on the ice roads, taking goods to the oil fields.'

'An ice road trucker?'

'Yep, though he must be crazy. My younger brother, Liam, is an architect, working abroad at the moment. He's trying to get planning permission to build a community on Barratt Island for those born here, but the town council are fighting him every step of the way. They like the island to be exclusively for the rich.'

'So are you the only brother who stayed home?'

'Why move from the most beautiful place on earth? Some people, like Julia — well, they never settle. They get an itch to move and they have to keep scratching it. Me, I've always known where I'm meant to be.'

'Do you think Julia and Merle will be okay?' Nell asked. 'I mean, they seemed a bit unhappy last night, and they're such a nice couple.' Nell realised she was waffling again, to cover up for her nosiness.

'People go through rough times. You must know that.'

Nell scoffed. 'I didn't get a chance to find out.'

'I don't understand.' Colm frowned.

'It's a long story.'

'It'll take us another half an hour to get to the mainland, and I'm not going anywhere. Unless you'd rather not tell me.'

'I've nothing to hide, Colm,' she said. 'I just don't want to bore you.'

'Nothing you've said so far has bored me.'

'I'm glad to hear it.' She took a deep breath. 'Rick and I dated for years. And I mean, years. I had my own house and he lived with his mum and dad. I kept hinting at marriage, or some sort of commitment, but he said they needed him, and I'm not the sort to give ultimatums. We drifted on like that for over ten years. Then Rick's mum and dad died, and we decided we might as well get married. There was no fanfare. No violins and sweeping music. We just booked the registry office then nipped out from work one afternoon — we both worked at the library — and did it, grabbing two people off the streets as witnesses. We hadn't even decided where we were going to live, so for the first week or so, Rick stayed put at his mum and dad's old house; just visiting me occasionally, and staying the night about once a week. After two weeks of this I thought that, as his wife, I'd perhaps earned the right to make ultimatums; so I told him he either moved in with me or it was over. That was when he told me that he'd fallen for the thirty-year-old nurse who used to care for his parents, and that he hadn't had the heart to tell me.' Nell laughed, but it had no humour. 'He had the heart to marry me and string me along, but not to tell me the truth about this girl. I don't even know what he told her. I gave up so much, waiting for him to make up his mind about me. I've come to the conclusion I may never have children now.' Nell sighed. 'Sometimes I ask myself why I waited so long. Nothing tied me to him, except my own apathy.'

'And love?' Colm suggested.

'Oh, love . . . I really have no idea what love is anymore. When I was younger I thought it was fireworks and violins, and then when I met Rick, I thought maybe it's just feeling comfortable with someone. Now I wonder if it's something completely different. Something I've never been able to feel. And that frightens me, because if I can't feel love for someone, then what am I?'

'You love your family. And that sister you told me about. Sandra?'

'Yes, I do. And my mum and dad if I'm honest. Oh, they're a bit set in their ways, and I was never the daughter they wanted me to be, but they're good people. But I mean passionate love. You know ... ' She looked up into his eyes and their gazes held for a long time. She jumped down off the seat, unnerved by the feelings raging in her heart. 'Oh, listen to me, boring you with my life story. Come on, tell me yours. You've at least earned the right to do that.'

'I've told you. I met Mary at school, we fell in love, and we married and had Kathleen when I was nineteen years old. Happy ever after.'

'Were you deeply in love? Fireworks, violins and all that?'

'Yes.'

'I'm glad, because you're a nice man and you deserve all that.' The pang Nell felt was nothing to do with jealousy. There was no point being jealous of a dead woman and she did not begrudge Colm his love for his late wife. It was right he should feel that way. The pang was more of an ache for something she had somehow missed in life. She felt the void stretching out in front of her, like the Atlantic Ocean.

'So do you, Nell.'

'Hmm . . . I think I'm too selfish and set in my ways now. I think that's why I wasn't exactly heartbroken when Rick left. I was more angry with myself for letting things go on for so long. I had the ability to change things, but I didn't.'

'Don't be so hard on yourself. The relationship with the nurse must have started before Rick's mom and dad died. He should have been honest with you.'

'You're so kind,' said Nell. Tears pricked her eyes. 'Oh dear, I'm getting old and silly now.'

'Old, never. Silly? Well, why not? We all deserve to be that now and then.'

'Oh, that's not the silliest thing in all this.'

'No?'

'No, I, er . . . Oh, it doesn't matter. I've come to get away from all that. Let's just have a nice evening and forget it all.'

'You're on!'

Colm moored the boat in a marina on the mainland where he seemed to be well known. In fact, he seemed to be known wherever they went.

Vinnie, the proprietor of the fish restaurant where they ate, had also been born on the island. The restaurant was built on stilts, stretching out over the water. The tables were covered in butcher paper, which Nell had never seen in a restaurant before. On a counter in the middle of the room, a life-size copper mermaid spread her arms out to the guests, as if welcoming them in. The room, which was lined with wood at the bottom of the walls and red bricks at the top, was dimly lit by rows of fairy lights stretching across the ceiling.

'I wanted to see the world,' Vinnie told Nell as he took their order. 'I left Barratt Island, landed here and this is as far as I've been since then. Still, I'm not complaining. The world comes to me instead, and now Colm brings me a beautiful English lady. How could I complain?'

'You silver-tongued charmer,' Nell said, blushing to the roots of her hair.

'What can I get for you, Lady Nell?' Vinnie teased. 'The scallops are good, but the surf and turf is the best in the district. I have to serve that, because if Colm goes a day without steak, he turns into a seven-stone weakling.'

'I'll bet,' said Nell, giggling.

'Or would you like to try some crab?

They're brought fresh here every morning. You can pick your own from the tank.' Vinnie gestured to the tank at the end of the room.

'Oh no, sorry,' said Nell. 'I couldn't eat something I'd looked in the eye.'

That made Vinnie laugh so much that he broke out into a fit of coughing. When he had calmed down, he said, 'Tell you what, why don't you try our crab sampler? It's got a bit of everything on it.'

'Okay, I'll try that, thank you.'

'I guess it's the surf and turf for you, Colm.'

'You guess wrong. I'll try the crab sampler too. The only reason I have the surf and turf is because it's the only thing you ever offer me in this lousy dump.'

'Lousy dump, yeah? Says a man who lives on donuts and black coffee.'

'Hey, I resent that stereotype about cops,' said Colm. He paused a beat and then grinned, winking at Nell. 'I like milk in my coffee.'

Vinnie gave him a playful flip around the head with his teatowel. 'Ha, funny guy. Nell, take it from me, you can't trust this man. He pretends to be this upstanding cop, pillar of the community and all that, but you should have known him at school. Public enemy number one in training, he was. Hey Colm, remember the time we ran the vice-principal's underwear up the flagpole? And that's not all . . .'

'Hey, hey,' said Colm. 'Save the character assassination for later. We're hungry here.'

Blissfully happy, Nell rested her chin on her hands. 'Everyone here is so friendly and warm,' she said. 'I've lived in the same village for years, yet we hardly speak to each other. I don't know one person I knew at school. Yet you and Vinnie are separated by three miles of ocean and still talk as if you last saw each other only yesterday.'

'Well, we did, when I had to bring a prisoner across to the courthouse.'

She waved her hand dismissively.

'Oh, you know what I mean.'

'Yeah, I know what you mean. Strange, I always imagine English villages to be like those in the crime shows. You know, Miss Marple, sticking her nose into everyone's business.'

Nell, who had just taken a sip of water, coughed and choked a little. 'Sorry, went down the wrong way,' she said. 'So, tell me all about Vinnie.'

They spent a pleasant evening chatting over a prolonged meal, which was interspersed with Vinnie coming over to tell Nell more of Colm's secrets. Though they were rather tame secrets, and the sort of things every teenage boy did at some point, Vinnie had a way of telling the stories that made them sound hilarious; and Colm's growing, but good-natured, embarrassment was great fun to behold.

'Hey,' said Vinnie as they were leaving. 'Is it true that Merle and Julia are living back on the island?'

'Yes, they are,' said Colm. 'Right across from Patty's house, in fact.'

'Yeah. That was a surprise, him leaving his wife like that.'

'These things happen, Vinnie,' Colm said, cautiously.

'Yeah, but for the Black Widow?'

'Come on, Vinnie, that isn't fair. We gotta go before it gets too late. See you again, pal.'

Nell had the sensation of being bundled away from the restaurant. She was dying to ask what was behind Vinnie's remarks, but Colm had seemed annoyed about them, and she did not want to spoil their evening by gossiping.

'Thank you,' she said, as they sailed back to the island in the moonlight. 'I've really enjoyed myself.'

'Yes, me too,' said Colm, smiling down at her as he steered the boat. 'We should do it again sometime.'

'That would be nice.'

'Nice?'

'Lovely. Enjoyable. Special. Whatever else happens in the next few months, Colm, I'm glad I got to spend some time with you.'

She fought the urge to kiss him, afraid of frightening him off, so she was surprised when his lips found hers instead. His arm stole around her waist, bringing her in closer as the kiss grew deeper. By the time he let her go she was more than a little breathless. Had he heard them too?, she wondered. The violins. She could have sworn that they swelled up from the sea, played by an underwater orchestra.

She put her head on his shoulder, deciding not to worry about that for now. Even if only she could hear them, she had proved herself capable of doing so.

When he moored the boat they held hands all the way back to Canopache, talking quietly but saying nothing much at all. When they reached the door, Nell turned and kissed him lightly on the lips. Should she invite him in? Would he think she was a bit too easy? She was seriously out of the dating habit, having drifted along with Rick for so long. Oh, what the hell! It was time to take hold of life, instead of letting it pass her by.

The question was on her lips when she heard someone scream Colm's name. It was Julia.

'Colm, Colm, come quickly.' Julia's voice broke into a sob. 'Merle is dead.'

5

It seemed fitting that it rained on the day of the funeral. Nell knew she did not have to go. After all, she barely knew Merle. Nevertheless, she thought it was right that she should attend.

Over a week had passed since that awful night when Colm had tried so hard to resuscitate Merle until the ambulance crew arrived. But everyone agreed it was too late. As Merle lay on the lounge floor, his face pallid, Colm had stood up with a bead of sweat on his brow.

'I'm sorry, Julia,' he said. He looked so crestfallen that Nell had to fight the compulsion to put her arms around him. It did not seem appropriate.

'You did your best, Colm,' said Julia, her eyes shining. Nell tried to decipher was what behind those eyes. There was admiration for Colm, that much was sure, but also something else. It must be grief, thought Nell. It had to be grief. Yet there was something missing . . .

'Tell me what happened,' said Colm, his policing instincts obviously taking over.

'I went out to get some supper for us, and when I returned, he was slumped in that chair.' Her voice was cool and mechanical. Almost as if she had rehearsed it.

'What time was this?'

'A few minutes before I called you.'

That could not be right, thought Nell. She and Colm had walked back from the harbour, but no cars had passed them in either direction.

'Did you walk?' she asked Nell, the words tumbling out before she could stop herself.

'What? Oh yes, I walked.'

'You must have been a few minutes ahead of us then,' said Nell, kicking herself for stating the obvious. Yet they had seen no one else on the road either.

62

She found herself looking around for evidence of the takeaway food that Julia was supposed to have brought with her, then mentally slapped herself for going down that road. She had made a fool of herself once, she would not do it again.

'Your point being?' said Julia, folding her arms defensively.

'That if we'd managed to catch up with you, we might have been able to do something for poor Merle sooner.' Nell's voice drifted away to nothing. The excuse sounded vapid even to her.

'I did try to resuscitate him,' Julia said, her eyes darkening.

'Of course.' Nell was beginning to wish she was somewhere else. Why did she have this propensity to start suspecting people of wrongdoing? Merle had been a very poorly man, that much was certain. Yet Nell remembered him enjoying Colm's rib eye steak only the night before. She also remembered his words about it feeling some days like he was dying.

She had heard that people often had a sense of fatality when death was near. Perhaps that was all it had been. But there had been something else about the way he enjoyed the food. As if he . . . trusted it.

'I should go and leave you to sort things out,' said Nell. 'I really am sorry about Merle, Julia. He was a very sweet man.'

'The best . . . ' said Julia, putting a tissue to her eyes.

But they were dry, Nell thought as she crossed the road back to her own house. There were no tears.

When she went back to Canopache, she took out her laptop and, ignoring her book on Montaigne, opened up a new Word file. She began to write down everything that had happened since arriving on the island. All of Julia's strange behaviour, and also how happy Merle had been at the barbecue, despite his ashen features. She mixed it with the story of her meeting Colm. She wrote for hours and hours, only giving in to sleep as the sun began to rise over the Atlantic.

★   ★   ★

Julia's eyes were not dry at the funeral. She spent much of it holding onto Colm, sobbing into his collar. Nell bit down on the sudden feeling of jealousy. It was right that he should console his old schoolfriend. He and Julia would have a lot in common now, with Colm having lost his wife. I have no claim on him, thought Nell, so what right do I have to be jealous? Still, the feelings would not die.

When the service was over and Merle's body had been interred, Nell wandered away from the group and looked around the churchyard. It was a pretty place with a white clapboard church, surrounded by picket fences, some of which overlooked the sea. There were a lot of Barratts named on the headstones, tracing the family back as far as the Civil War era. The first seemed to be a Samuel Barratt, who was interred with his wife Amelia.

Nell had not asked much about the history of the island, but it seemed as if the Barratts actually owned it, and had done for a long time. She found Mary Barratt's gravestone, which, appropriately, had the statue of an angel. The grave had been regularly tended. It was odd, she thought, how she did not feel jealous of Colm's wife, who had obviously been the love of his life, yet she felt jealous of Julia. *Because Julia is here*, that small nagging voice inside her said. And because Julia needed him now she was alone.

Nell also found a few Silkwoods, going back almost as far as the Barratts. She wondered what Julia's maiden name had been. One man was called Joshua Silkwood.

'My great-grandfather,' a quiet voice said beside her. She turned to see a young woman whom she had noticed earlier. The girl had held herself back from the rest of the crowd, almost as if she did not want to be seen. With hair that had been coloured jet-black, Goth-style make-up and a long black silk dress, it would have been difficult *not* to notice her.

'You're a relative of Merle's?' asked Nell. 'I'm afraid I didn't know him well, but he seemed to be a very nice man.'

'He was until she got hold of him,' the girl said bitterly. 'I'm his daughter, Ruby.'

'Oh, I didn't realise Merle had children. I'm so sorry for your loss. Is Julia your mother?' Nell was sure that Julia had told her she and Merle had no children.

'Dear God, no!' Ruby scoffed. 'My mom is on the mainland. She wanted to come, but Julia warned her away. Anyone would think Mom was responsible for breaking up the marriage, when everyone knows it was that witch.'

'Oh.'

'Is she your friend? Julia, I mean? Because if she is and you have a husband, for God's sake keep a close eye on him. Especially if he has money'

'I'm sorry you've been hurt. I think Julia has been too.' Why Nell was defending Julia she did not know, but she felt she owed her some loyalty. 'She's lost two husbands now. And you've lost a father.'

The girl snorted. 'Two? Is that what she's told you? Try four.'

'Four husbands?' Nell's eyes widened in surprise.

'Oh, yes. They don't call her the Black Widow for nothing.'

'Ruby!' A voice cracked out across the churchyard. 'I do hope you're not going to cause any trouble. It is your father's funeral, after all.' Julia, dressed in an expensive black suit, was walking towards them. Colm followed a few feet behind.

Nell put her hand on Ruby's arm, protectively. 'She's not causing trouble, Julia. She's just come to say goodbye to her father.'

'Ruby,' said Colm, overtaking Julia. 'I'm sorry, I didn't realise who you were. I haven't seen you since you were this high.' He gestured to a height just above his left knee. 'I don't suppose you remember me.'

'Uncle Colm,' Ruby said, her voice trembling. 'Yes, I remember you. It's good to see you again.'

'You too, honey. I just wish it could have been under different circumstances. Why don't you come up to the house? We're holding the wake at my place, because Julia doesn't feel up to doing it at hers.'

'Hers?' Ruby scoffed.

'I'm sure Ruby needs to get back to the mainland before night-time,' said Julia. 'As it's high season, there won't be anywhere for her to stay on the island.'

'She could stay with me,' Nell interposed. 'I mean, if Colm thinks Patty wouldn't mind.'

'I'm sure Patty would be glad you were taking care of a friend's daughter,' said Colm, his eyes signalling his appreciation.

'I'm staying at Canopache,' she

explained to Ruby. 'There are far too many rooms there for just me. You'd be very welcome.'

'Thank you,' said Ruby, casting a glance at Julia. 'But Julia is right. I should get back to the mainland. I promised Mom I wouldn't be long.'

'How is Barbara?' asked Colm.

'How do you think?' Ruby snapped. Then, more gently: 'Sorry, Uncle Colm. She's okay. Just a little sad, you know?'

'I'll come over and see you both in the week,' Colm promised.

'Thank you ... erm ... ' Ruby turned to Nell and held out her hand. 'I'm sorry, I don't know your name.'

'Nell Palmer.'

'Thank you for your offer, Ms Palmer.'

'Call me Nell, and consider it an open offer whilst I'm staying here,' Nell insisted. 'If you ever want to come over here and, oh, I don't know, see the places your dad used to go, to help you remember him, then you're welcome to stay.'

As Ruby walked away from them, her eyes straight ahead as if determined not to look at Julia, Nell felt tears of sympathy sting her eyes. The girl had lost her father, and yet she was being treated like an outsider. An interloper.

'I'm glad she's gone,' said Julia, tight-lipped. 'She insists on blaming me for everything, whereas I always say that if a couple are happy then nothing can come between them. Clearly Barbara and Merle weren't happy. I'm just glad I was able to bring some joy to the poor man's life.'

Nell almost wanted to laugh. Whatever Merle had been feeling in the last few days of his life, it was not joy. But people had a way of rewriting history when someone died. No doubt Julia was doing it to make herself feel better for whatever problems she and Merle might have had whilst he was alive. Nell could hardly blame her for that, yet still her sympathies were for the young girl — no more than a child — who had just walked away alone.

'I, er . . . I just need to get something in town before I come up to your place,' she said to Colm, dashing off before he could protest.

Wiping the tears from her eyes, Nell raced after Ruby. The girl was younger, so much quicker than Nell. She was already sitting on the dock when Nell, completely out of breath, got there. Ruby sat on a crate, biting the black varnish from her fingernails.

'Ruby . . . ' Nell said. 'I don't want to intrude, but I'd really like to come and talk to you sometime. If it's no intrusion.'

'If you come next week, I'll introduce you to my mom. But not now. She's too upset.'

'Yes, I can understand that. I'll come next week. Tell me where you live.'

Ruby scribbled her address on a piece of scrap paper from Nell's handbag. 'It's not far from the harbour. A couple of blocks from Vinnie's seafood place. Do you know it?'

'Yes, I know it. I was there last week

with Colm. The night your dad was . . . the night he died.'

Ruby turned out to be very smart indeed. 'You were going to say 'the night he was murdered', weren't you?'

'No, of course not. Don't be silly. Not that your fears are silly. I mean, no, I wasn't going to say that.'

A siren signalled the arrival of the ferry for the mainland. Ruby started walking up the gangplank. 'Maybe you should find out about her other husbands before we talk again,' she called back to Nell when she reached the top.

6

Colm's house was open-plan down-stairs, with the living room off an arched entrance from the hallway; on the other side, also through an archway, was a dining room. The table was laden with food, and waiters, hired for the day, made sure everyone had a glass of sherry.

Julia moved from guest to guest, taking their sympathy, and then ensuring they had enough food.

'Anyone would think it was her house,' Wendy muttered to Nell.

'I suppose it is her husband's wake,' said Nell, trying to find the good in Julia and failing.

'Oh, you're too nice.'

'Not really. Did you see Merle's daughter, Ruby, at the funeral?'

'Oh, the Goth girl? Yes. Though I didn't know who she was until someone pointed her out to me. Poor kid.'

'Is it true . . . ' Nell lowered her voice. 'Is it true that Julia has been married four times?'

'Oh, so you found out. Yes, it's true. And she's traded up each time. I think she's really going for it for husband number five.' Wendy cast a glance in Colm's direction. 'Since William Barratt died last year, his sons and daughter are in a good financial position.'

Colm was standing by the fireplace, talking to an elderly woman whom Nell had learned was one of Merle's aunts. The woman seemed to be rather irate, and Colm appeared to be doing his best to calm her down.

'But she's his daughter,' the woman's voice rang out.

Nell could not hear Colm's response, but his lips made an 'I know, I know' movement as he touched the woman gently on the shoulder.

'Julia only told me she'd had one previous husband,' Nell said.

'She has a very selective memory,'

said Wendy. 'In her mind, she and Colm should have got together at school, and would have if not for Mary. Oh, I'm sorry; I know you two have been dating.'

'We've had one date,' Nell corrected her. 'I'm not in a position to claim him.'

Wendy pursed her lips. 'Let's have a coffee later this week and talk properly. It's not easy to do so here.'

Nell hung around for another ten minutes, until she felt she had paid her respects enough, and then quietly slipped away. Halfway down the pathway from Colm's house, she took off her shoes, and decided she would not be sorry to change the dark dress she wore into something more summery.

'Hey, you escaping?'

She turned to see Colm walking down the path after her. She waited until he was abreast of her before answering.

'I feel as if I'm intruding,' she said, which was not strictly a lie.

'No, it's good that you came. You

didn't have to, but it was the right thing to do. I'm sure Julia appreciates it.'

It was on Nell's mind to say that she had not attended for Julia's sake. Instead she said, 'Merle was a nice man. It's ridiculous but I keep thinking about how much he enjoyed that steak and beer at your place the night before he died. The way he smacked his lips as if it was the best meal he'd ever had.'

'Yes, me too. I feel bad about Ruby,' Colm said, running his fingers through his hair. 'I should have gone to see her and Barbara after Merle died. I just didn't think.'

'You've had a busy week helping Julia to deal with everything.'

'Yeah, I guess so. I'm sorry it means that we haven't spent more time together. You and me, I mean.'

'I understand.'

'Was Ruby okay when you caught up with her at the dock?'

How had he known that? 'Yes, she was fine. Or as well as she could be.'

'I'm glad someone showed her some sympathy. I've just had Merle's aunt tell me off for not looking after her better. But I honestly didn't recognise her.'

'Well, to be fair, Merle's aunt could have taken care of her,' said Nell. 'But no one spoke to her.'

'I hadn't looked at it that way. Mind you, Ruby's changed since she was a little girl. She used to have bright auburn hair, like my daughter Kathleen. We're all related, you know, somewhere way back when.'

'Is that why she called you Uncle Colm?'

'I guess so, though really we're more like distant cousins ten times removed. That sort of thing. I'll go and see her and her mom this week. Barbara must be feeling awful. She never stopped loving Merle.'

'What happened, Colm? Between Merle and Barbara and Julia?'

'I don't want to gossip. Anyway, that's not why I came out here. I just wanted to know if you'd have dinner with me again tomorrow night. Hopefully Julia will be okay now, and we can get back to what we started. If you want to.'

'Are you sure that's what you want?' asked Nell.

'Yeah, of course. I've been neglecting you this week, and I promised Patty I'd . . . ' He hesitated. 'Take care of you.'

'I'm a big girl, Colm. I don't need a babysitter.' Nell had the distinct impression that he had been about to say something else.

'I like spending time with you, but if you'd rather . . . '

'I like being with you too,' Nell said hastily. 'I'm not ungrateful. I just don't want to infringe on your time.' Before she could say anymore, she saw Julia appear at the top of the path.

'Colm, honey, our guests are leaving,' Julia called.

'You're needed and I'd better go,' Nell said.

She turned and flew down the path,

forgetting about the rocks on her bare feet. Julia had already staked her claim on Colm, and Nell did not think she could ever compete.

7

Nell spent the next week avoiding Colm as much as she could. She went out early in the morning, either over onto the mainland, or exploring the wildlife sanctuary to the north of the island. She would only return late in the day, collapsing into a chair and wishing she was back in her own little cottage.

So much for a place of peace! She had walked into a situation that she could not control. Her feelings would not let her. But Colm and Julia had a history. It was natural they should find solace in each other. The fact that Nell did not like Julia was beside the point. She had probably not seen the woman at her best. Taking care of Merle must have put a huge strain on her. Not everyone was a natural nurse, and Nell had once had a workmate who was a darling to everyone in the library, but had no patience for her sick husband. It took Nell a while to realise that her workmate was afraid of losing him, and that this manifested itself in her bad moods. The woman's true feelings only came out when the man died.

Julia certainly seemed to be relieved of that pressure every time Nell saw her around the town. She was either coming out of the haberdashers' with curtain material or overseeing the unloading of new furniture from a boat. All the strain had gone from her face, and Nell began to see how attractive Julia Silkwood was.

All the spending only added to Nell's suspicions, but she was afraid to voice them to anyone. She had made that mistake before. This time, she would find out the truth before getting in touch with the police. And there was the rub. Colm *was* the police on Barratt Island. How could she go to him and tell him that a woman he had known for most of his life might have killed her husband?

The inquest into Merle's death had said he died of the effects of gastric flu, which he had been suffering from for some time. She looked up arsenic on the Internet and learned that it could cause gastric problems. 'But surely they would have found it in the autopsy,' she murmured to herself. Did any police department expect a man to die from arsenic poisoning in this day and age? It was the stuff of Agatha Christie novels, and turn-of-the-twentieth-century women out to make money from their husbands' life insurance policies. Merle had come into a lot of money after his accident. Nell had no idea how much, but she supposed it must be a lot if Merle and Julia could afford to buy a house on the island and still live a comfortable existence.

In the middle of the week, Nell decided to hop on the ferry to the mainland. It was too soon to visit Ruby and her mother, but Vinnie at the seafood restaurant might be able to shed some light on Julia's life before she married Merle.

She spent the morning looking at more Civil War monuments and a small museum devoted to the war. It seemed the Barratts had played a big part in that too. Colm's ancestors were listed among the dead, but also among those who were given honours. Samuel Barratt, whose grave she had seen, had gone to West Point and risen to the rank of General. It turned out the island had been given to him by a grateful nation, and had been in the Barratt family ever since. Nell had once looked up her own family history, and found she could only trace them back to farm labourers. Ah well, she thought, people needed to eat as well as win wars. But it all made her feel that she would never fit into Colm's life.

Insisting that it did not matter, but knowing full well she was lying to herself, she went to Vinnie's for lunch.

'Why, it's Lady Nell,' said Vinnie. He made a great flourish and showed her to a table on the deck overlooking the sea. There were a few people eating at other tables, but the restaurant was not busy. 'Alone today?'

'Yes. I've been looking at the Civil War museum.'

'Where's Colm?'

'I've no idea. Catching criminals on Barratt Island, I suppose.'

Vinnie burst out laughing. 'Yeah, like it's a real den of iniquity over there.'

'They must have some crime or they wouldn't need policemen.'

'True, true. I think the worst of it is drunken holidaymakers, and the occasional burglary, usually by someone from the mainland.'

'No murders?' said Nell, watching Vinnie's face for a reaction.

His eyes seemed to shade for a moment. 'I guess there must have been at some time. Why, you got any suspicions?' He handed her a menu.

It seemed to be Vinnie's turn to watch her for a reaction. 'It was very sad about Merle Silkwood, wasn't it?'

she said. It was hardly changing the subject, but she wanted to know if Vinnie had any suspicions.

'Yeah, I'm sorry I didn't make it for the funeral, but I had a chef off sick and I couldn't leave this place. How is Julia?'

'She's, erm . . . fine, I think. She seems to be doing a bit of refurbishing.'

'Really? That's interesting. What can I get you to drink, Lady Nell?'

'Just mineral water, please. Vinnie?'

'Yeah?'

'Do you know Julia's maiden name? It's just I've been very interested in the island, and the people on it. I've learned all about Colm's family. I wondered where her family fit into it all.'

'Now you're asking. Julia's family were immigrants, like mine, though not Italian. They came over in the early nineteen-hundreds. Again like mine. They're from somewhere in Eastern Europe. Yanev was the name, I think. That's it. Julia Yanev. They didn't move to the island until the nineteen-sixties, and then only so her mom could clean for the Barratts. This was when old man Barratt and his wife were alive. But old Mrs Yanev, Julia's mother, she was a strange one. She always insisted the family were related to royalty and that cleaning was beneath her. I honestly don't know why Colm's mom and dad put up with her. She was always in a foul mood, couldn't cook, and didn't always keep the house as clean as she might have. I think Mrs Barratt felt sorry for her. Whatever the truth of her past, the Yanevs had obviously been through some bad stuff.'

'So did Julia grow up thinking she was royalty?'

'Oh yeah. When we were in school she'd tell us she was a princess. But it got her mocked rather than admired, so after a while she shut up about it.'

'Poor Julia. I mean, if it was her mother's lie . . . '

'Yeah, I guess. Now, what can I get you to eat?'

'Could I just have fish and chips?'

'The great old English treat, eh? It'll be right up. Hey, I'll even serve them in newspaper if you want.'

'That's not allowed anymore. Health and safety and all that rubbish.'

'Really? Gee, I always wanted to come to England and eat proper fish and chips out of the *Daily Mail*.'

Nell wanted to talk to Vinnie more, but the restaurant started to fill up and she did not want to infringe on his time. Now she had Julia's maiden name, she could start looking into her other marriages.

The fish and chips were delicious. Better than any she had ever tasted. She finished it off with a slice of banoffee pie.

'At this rate I'm going to have to charter a cargo plane to take me home,' she told Vinnie as she paid the bill.

He waved away her tip. 'You don't have to tip me,' he said. 'You're a friend of Colm's.'

Nell smiled awkwardly. 'Thank you.'

She stood up to leave and he insisted on escorting her to the door.

'Vinnie?' she said.

'Yeah?'

'Did you know Julia had been married four times?'

'That's a rough estimate,' he said, raising an eyebrow.

'What?'

'She went away from here for a while, and then returned looking like she had money.'

'She might have earned it,' said Nell.

'Oh yeah, she earned it alright.' Vinnie winked.

'Vinnie, you're incorrigible.'

'I ain't got a clue what that means so I'll just agree with you,' he said.

'Oh, I think you know,' said Nell. 'The simple-immigrant act doesn't work on me, you know.'

Vinnie laughed. 'I'll remember that! You take care now, Lady Nell, and don't let Julia queer your pitch.'

'What do you mean?'

'She's had her eye on Colm Barratt

for a long time, but that doesn't mean she's right for him. If she was, I reckon they'd have been married a long time ago, don't you?'

'Sometimes people wait,' said Nell. 'Because they're afraid of admitting their feelings or of rushing into something.'

'Colm wouldn't wait. The Barratts have learned how to get what they want in life. Oh, they do it with that charming smile, and because they're good people they get away with it, but don't mistake that down-home charm for weakness. If Colm wanted Julia, he'd have married her, just as he did Mary.'

Nell wanted to believe that what Vinnie said was right; but sometimes people who had known each other a long time got together because they were comfortable with each other. That Julia had her heart set on Colm was without doubt. But did Colm have his heart set on Julia?

Nell only knew that she had never

felt that same tingle when her ex-husband kissed her. Colm's kiss held the promise of a passion that had been missing in her life. But one kiss did not mean that Colm was, or ever would be, devoted to her.

★　★　★

Colm drove up to Canopache, hoping to find Nell in. He feared that, with her not being from the area, she would not have watched the local news — which had given out a severe storm warning. At least, that was the excuse he gave himself. In reality, he wanted to know how she was, and why she appeared to be avoiding him.

He was smart enough to realise it had something to do with Julia; but in his mind, Julia was just an old friend in need of comfort. If he could just explain that to Nell, everything would be okay.

'Colm!'

He turned to see Wendy walking up

from the town. 'Colm, I've been wanting to talk to you.'

'Hi Wendy. What's the problem?'

'Oh, nothing much. I'm on my way up to see my daughter. But I saw you, and thought I'd ask you about something that's been worrying me. You know I've been doing the stock-taking for old man Wharton at the plant nursery?'

'Yeah.'

'Well, I picked up on something a bit odd, and I just wanted to run it by you . . .'

'Colm, I'm sorry, I didn't know you were calling on me today.' Julia's voice rang out across the street, surprising both Colm and Wendy. Colm turned, frowning. His car was outside Canopache, not Julia's house, so why had she assumed he was calling on her? 'I just called to warn Nell about the incoming storm,' he said, kindly but firmly.

'Well, now you're here, could you help me? I've got some paperwork about Merle's will and I'm not so good with the legal jargon. I figured you being a cop . . . '

'Could you wait a moment, Julia? I think Wendy wanted to talk to me.' Colm bit back a feeling of irritation. He wanted to help Julia, but felt she was becoming a bit too dependent upon him. He silently chided himself for feeling that way. After all, she had just lost her husband, and he should be supporting his childhood friend. But he was coming to realise that Julia wanted more than that. If he was not careful, he might find it hard to shake her off.

'It's okay, Colm,' said Wendy, biting her lip. 'I'll come see you down at the station.'

Colm tipped his hat to Wendy and walked across to Julia's. He wanted to be a good friend, but something in his mind screamed at him to run as fast as he could.

He stole a look back at Canopache, its windows and doors all closed up. He had a key, his sister had given it to him before she went away; but it was Nell's place for the summer and he did not want to intrude.

Julia stood at her door, which was wide open. It was odd how that felt more forbidding than Canopache's locked doors.

* * *

Nell popped into an Internet café and did a search for Julia Yanev. A picture from a school yearbook came up in the image search: of a plain young girl, with wild nineteen-eighties hair swept back in a scrunchie and braces on her teeth. Another image showed her as a bride in New York State, with a groom called Roger Harris, who was clearly many years older than Julia. She must have been about nineteen or twenty at the time. She had blossomed from a plain teenager into a very attractive young woman.

Nell searched for Roger Harris, and found an obituary notice showing that Roger Harris had died only a couple of years after their marriage of 'natural causes', leaving a 'loving wife' Julia, and two grown-up children by his first marriage. He was sixty-six years old and had owned a car dealership. Her next search was for the widowed Julia Harris, who had married a man called Hank Black in Texas. He too was much older, and he had also died within a couple of years of them marrying. Hank had owned his own stables which, according to the report, had produced horses that won the Kentucky Derby and Grand National.

The news about Julia moved closer to home, as presumably she did, and Nell found evidence of at least two more husbands in the New England area. One had definitely died, but there was no news of the other man. Each of the men had been well-to-do, even if they were not super-rich; and with each marriage, Julia had advanced her life — and moved closer to Barratt Island. The most up-to-date wedding picture was of Julia and Merle, but the bride had resumed using the name Julia Harris before she married him. Nell wondered if Merle even knew about all Julia's husbands.

Another newspaper report prior to their wedding discussed Merle's accident in a mainland factory, about five years previously, which resulted in his hands being crushed. The report said that Merle was expecting to receive a million-dollar settlement due to the company's negligence. That was less than a year before Merle married Julia. The picture accompanying the article showed Merle and a homely-looking woman sitting on a sofa, their heads together. The caption said it was him and his wife Barbara. Merle had been bigger then. Not fat, but healthy-looking, despite his injuries. The couple had looked right together, Nell thought. They were a couple who had been through a lot but come out of it stronger. Or they should have.

Nell found a similar article with the same picture on another news site. In that report, Barbara talked about how others had helped them. 'We're blessed with good friends,' she said. 'Our neighbour, Julia, has been around every day to see what she can do for us, and she takes care of Merle when I have to go out.'

'I bet she did,' Nell muttered to herself. Julia had followed the money and ended up back where she had always wanted to be. On Barratt Island. Nell could not blame her for that. The island held a strange hold over people. Even Vinnie had not moved too far away, and Barratt Island could be seen from the seafood restaurant. Now Julia had set her cap at Colm. Was it because she had spent all of Merle's money? Or did she just want to trade up to an even richer husband?

Nell closed down the computer and left the café, telling herself that it was none of her business. Colm was a big boy and could take care of himself. It was just Julia's track record that bothered her. The woman's husbands had a habit of dying, or disappearing from society, and that worried Nell. Merle worried Nell too. He had been thin and very unhappy, until he ate that steak at Colm's the night before he died.

It was as if . . . Without realising, Nell said the words out loud as she wandered down the street: ' . . . as if he knew he was being poisoned at home.' But if he believed that, why not go to the police? Why not refuse to eat anything that Julia fed him?

On the ferry ride back to the island, with the lush greenery of the New England forests behind her and the craggy rocks of Barratt Island ahead, she fell into thinking of Colm wasting away as Julia sapped the life out of him with poisoned food. It made her want to cry. He was so strong and handsome and vibrant, she could not bear to think of him being hurt. But what could she do? If she went to him and voiced her suspicions, he would think her mad. She needed more evidence, but how could she get it?

By the time she reached the island it was starting to get dark, and she had come to the decision to do a bit of detective work in the area. Besides, it would be fun to play detective. Maybe she could even redeem herself over the Mr Kemp debacle.

She would find out about Julia Silkwood — nee Yanev, nee Harris, nee-whatever-her-other-husbands-had-been — and only then, when Nell had proof, would she go to the police. But perhaps not Colm. She could not bear his look of disgust when she talked about her suspicions. Julia was his friend and he would surely have divided loyalties.

When she reached Canopache, it had started to rain and the wind whipped around her as she unlocked the door. Out over the sea was a thick black cloud, heralding a storm. She had reached home just in time.

As she turned to shut the front door, she saw Julia's front door open across the way. Colm came out, followed by

Julia, who put her arms around his neck and pulled his head down to hers.

Nell did not see anything else, because she slammed the door shut with a bang and locked it tightly. Serves him right, she thought angrily. He would be a fool if he fell for the Black Widow over there. Some men just deserved everything they got . . .

Even as she thought it, she knew that it was not true; and whether Colm cared for her or not, she would do everything she could to save him from the same fate as Merle.

8

The rain lashed against the windows and the wind rattled around the house. Nell had never known a storm like it. The very foundations of the house seemed to shake and she feared it may not survive the storm. She imagined herself as Dorothy Gale, being swept off into another world; though she knew that if the storm became a twister and took the house with it, all that waited for her was death.

'Silly woman,' she said to herself as she sat at the window seat in the kitchen, looking out over the bay. There was not much to see, yet normally at this time of night one could make out the lights from the mainland.

Every now and then fork lightning split the night sky, followed by a roll of thunder. Nell had always found thunderstorms rather exciting; while her sister had always hidden in the cupboard under the stairs whenever they happened, Nell had always had to be prevented from going out into the garden to see them at close hand.

It thundered again; three loud bangs that almost made her jump out of her skin. Only when another three loud bangs shook the house did she realise that someone was at the front door.

Who on earth . . . ? She went to the door and opened it to find a rain-sodden Colm standing there. His wavy hair was plastered to his forehead, and drops of rain hung off his dark eyelashes. 'You need to close the shutters,' he said, his breath coming in short bursts. 'If the windows break, the house will be full of glass. I'll help you.' Without being asked he barged inside. Nell almost protested, and then remembered that she was the guest and it was his sister's home. He had a right to protect it.

She followed him as he went from room to room downstairs, closing the shutters against the storm. Why had she not thought of that? Feeling rather foolish, Nell went upstairs and started doing the same in the bedrooms and bathrooms. As she did so, the lights began to flicker. She had closed the last shutter when everything went pitch-black. Outside, the lightning still struck and the thunder rolled. Closing the shutters had not stopped the house from shaking, and the vibrations seemed even more frightening in the darkness. She loved storms, but she had never been in one quite as powerful as this.

'Colm!' she cried, standing in the main bedroom, unsure what to do next. She saw a flicker of light on the landing and Colm appeared in the door, holding a candle. 'I'm sorry,' she stammered. 'You must think me very stupid. We don't have storms like this in Britain. Well, not often.'

'I came earlier to warn you, but you were out.' He walked into the room, and they were both encompassed in the glow from the candle.

'I went to the mainland for the day,' she explained, hoping he could not see her blush in the dim light. She did not want him to know what she had been up to.

'And I've been knocking for about five minutes.'

'You have? I thought you were with ... I thought it was the storm, I suppose.'

'Are you alright?' He put his hand on her shoulder. 'You're trembling.'

'Like I said, we don't have storms like this in Britain very often. When we do, we're dreadfully unprepared for them. You seem to have it all in hand.' She felt his hand caress her shoulder, and a tingle of pleasure ran down her spine.

'Would you like a drink?' she asked, looking up at him.

'Not really.' He appeared to move closer to her, looming over her in the dark. It was not an unpleasant feeling.

'Something to eat, then? I could

make sandwiches.'

'I'm not hungry, Nell.'

'Okay. Well, perhaps we should go downstairs until the storm passes.'

He lowered his head, his lips tantalisingly close to hers. She could smell the rain on his skin, and a droplet fell from his hair onto her forehead, giving her shivers. Unthinking, she reached up and brushed his damp fringe back. His free hand stole around her waist, pulling her in close, and then his lips sought hers. He tasted of the storm and the sea and she lapped him up hungrily.

He put the candle down and led her to the bed, where he gently stripped her naked. She pulled off his wet clothes, and pressed her warm body against his damp skin, tingling at the contrast. She gave up all her inhibitions and let him make love to her. The raging storm outside matched their passion note for note, until all was spent, leaving nothing but peace and contentment.

* * *

In the morning, Nell and Colm surveyed the damage. Patty's garden had taken a pasting, but Nell was relieved to see that her own heart had survived the storm.

She eyed Colm shyly over the breakfast table.

'How do you manage to do that?' he asked.

'Do what?'

'Go back to looking like a prim and proper librarian after last night?'

'It's a gift,' she said, her eyes shining. There was something she needed to know. 'Colm?'

'What, darling?'

She became flustered at the endearment. 'About Julia . . . I saw you kissing her. I know I have no right to question what you do. After all, last night might have meant nothing to you . . . '

'Do you really believe that?'

'I . . . I don't know. I don't think so. What I'm trying to say is that I don't expect any promises. I accept that last night was what it was . . . a one-off. I'm not going to go all bunny-boiler on you. In case you were worried.'

'First of all, you didn't see me kissing Julia, you saw her kissing me. Secondly, I don't do one-night stands. I never have, never will.'

'Oh.'

He got down from his stool and walked around the counter to her, putting his arm around her shoulder, his warm lips brushing her bare shoulder, 'And just to prove it, why don't we go upstairs and check the shutter in the bedroom? Who knows what might happen whilst we're up there?'

'Who knows indeed?' said Nell, a wave of pleasure washing over her.

She looked back on that day as one of the happiest of her life. She and Colm did very little but make love, eat, make love, eat more, then sleep peacefully after yet more love-making. She forgot about everything else. No one else in the world mattered.

'Don't you have criminals to catch?' she asked, as they lay snuggled together in the massive bed.

'Even I'm allowed a day off.'

'But after the storm . . . There might be looting or something.' She felt his body vibrate with laughter.

'Maybe in New York or Central London, but not here on Barratt Island. People here are generally well-behaved, apart from a couple of drunks now and then. Sometimes there's the odd burglary whilst people are away from home, but not often.'

'Haven't you ever had a nice juicy murder to investigate?'

'Once or twice.'

'You're probably going to laugh now,' she said. 'But . . . well, I've been investigating Julia. I know it's really stupid, but something told me that she'd poisoned Merle.' Nell told him about everything she had found out. She was so engrossed in her story that she did not notice that his body had become rigid. 'I think it's just because I was jealous of her, which I know makes me a dreadful person.'

Colm moved her hand, which had been draped over his bare chest, and sat up. 'I can't believe you did that!' he said. He got out of bed and pulled his trousers on.

'I know, and I've admitted it was silly of me.'

'Damn it, Nell, I . . . I wanted you to be different. I told Patty that she was wrong about you, that it was a misunderstanding with your neighbour, yet . . . you really do see murderers everywhere, don't you?'

'No, Colm. Listen.'

'I've heard enough.' He ran his hands through his hair. 'Really, Nell. Enough already. Just because we don't have looting and murder, doesn't mean we don't know how to do our jobs. Do you really think we're so dumb here that we wouldn't investigate a sudden death? Merle's test results just haven't come back yet. But I can't believe they'll show anything. If there was anything wrong, I'd have noticed.'

Aware of her nakedness, Nell threw on a t-shirt and her jeans. They stood on opposite sides of the bed, the thing that had brought them together now like an ocean of space dividing them. 'Oh, and you don't think her going buying up half the furniture shop is strange? Or setting her cap at you with her husband barely cold in his grave?'

'She has not set her cap at me, as you say. She's just been a woman in need of a friend.' Even as he said it, Nell saw a hint of doubt in his eyes. If she could only make him see sense!

'Then you are dumb, Colm, because she's wanted you since you were at school together. Everyone knows that.'

'No, Nell, everyone *doesn't* know that. People might think they know it, but ... Oh, I'm not having this argument. I really like you. We might have even been more to each other, but ... well, there's something wrong with you, and I don't know if I can deal with whatever issues you've got.'

'There's nothing wrong with me. I might have been wrong about Mr Kemp, but . . . ' Tears splashed Nell's cheeks. She had never felt so small or humiliated. 'Perhaps you'd better go.'

'Yeah, perhaps I should.'

Colm left the bedroom. Nell followed him, almost wanting to beg him to stay and to forget everything that had been said, but his words had hurt her too much. He saw her as some mad, lonely woman who made up stories about people. But she was not like that. Not at all!

As Colm walked down the stairs, his mobile phone rang. He took it out of his pocket, barking into it. Nell pitied the person on the other side. But Colm stopped halfway down the stairs, his whole manner changed. 'Jesus . . . Poor Wendy. I don't know what to say. I'll be there right away.'

'What is it?' asked Nell. He glared up at her. 'Please, Colm, whatever you might think of me, I like Wendy. I want to know what's happened to her.'

'The storm has destroyed once side of her house. She was found unconscious in the debris. She's in a helicopter on the way to the mainland, but they don't think she's going to wake up again. Damn it, I'm the police chief. I should have been out there helping people last night, instead of . . . '

Nell closed her eyes to stem the pain, but it was useless. His words had cut too deep. 'Yes,' she said. 'Yes, you should have.'

9

Wendy lay hooked up to a life-support machine in a hospital on the mainland. Nell had visited every day since Wendy's accident, doing her best to help the family by sitting with the patient whilst Ted went to get food and coffee. He had been stuck on the mainland during the storm, and their teenage daughter Kelly had been sleeping over at a friend's house.

'I shouldn't have left her,' said Ted. 'My trip wasn't even important.'

'It could have happened at any time,' Nell said soothingly. 'Wendy's a grown woman. She wouldn't have expected you to be with her all the time.'

Ted agreed there was sense in that, but she could still see the guilt in his eyes.

Nell felt bad that Wendy had been lying there in the house, whilst she and

Colm had spent the day making love. But, deep down, she knew that was no one's fault either, even if Colm was angry with her about it.

She had only seen him sporadically since that day, and always in the company of others. For a man who did not believe in one-night stands, he seemed to have quickly decided that that was all he and Nell had shared. For her part, she did not push him to make a commitment. It was obviously over between them, and Nell was determined not to be clingy. Soon she would be returning home and she could forget about him. That thought was like a knife hacking at her heart, but it was the only way forward.

Julia was also a regular visitor to the hospital, and appeared very concerned about Wendy. Nell wished she could bring herself to like the woman, but even when Julia was being caring, she had a cold, clinical way about her that made Nell distrust her motives.

Nell was so tied up with visiting

Wendy that she almost forgot about Ruby and Barbara Silkwood, until she received a phone call from Ruby, inviting her over to their house. Although she did not want to start investigating Julia again, she did not want to brush Ruby off; so, one Sunday afternoon, a couple of weeks after Wendy's accident, she took herself off to the mainland and to the small community in which Ruby and Barbara lived.

It was a street of single-storey wooden houses, not as upmarket as those on Barratt Island. The area had a rundown look about it, with overgrown yards and peeling paintwork on the houses, suggesting a low-income population. These, Nell guessed, were the people who kept the more affluent communities comfortable by working in the stores, serving the coffees or cleaning the multi-million dollar villas that stretched along the coast line.

'They call this place Barren Island,' Ruby told her as they sat around the lunch table. Barbara had cooked a pot roast with fresh vegetables, and it was delicious. 'But living in the projects here is still one hundred times better than living in the projects in New York, so we don't complain.'

'Not that Julia ever thought so,' said Barbara. She was a small, ample-figured woman with warm brown eyes that spoke of a Hispanic heritage. 'She hated it here.'

'How did she end up here?' asked Nell. 'I thought she married well, inheriting money from her husbands.'

'Yes, and she knew how to spend it,' said Barbara. 'She always said that living in Barren Island was just a stopping-off place until her fortunes improved and she got back to Barratt Island. Well, her fortunes didn't improve, but Merle's did when he had his accident. Do you know that she was the one who pushed him to sue the company? He wasn't bothered. He said 'accidents happen', but Julia was adamant he deserved something. What she really meant was that *she* deserved something. By the time he won his settlement, she'd whispered in his ear long enough to convince him that I didn't love him and that Ruby wasn't his daughter.' Barbara looked lovingly at the girl. 'She's every bit his daughter. Then Julia used Merle's money to buy her way back onto Barratt Island.'

'I don't understand,' said Nell. 'Since you were married, how come you didn't get anything in the divorce settlement?'

'We weren't married,' said Barbara, quietly. 'I took Merle's name, and called myself his wife, but we always said we didn't need a piece of paper.' She laughed harshly. 'Little did I know! I know it sounds materialistic of me, but I was so angry about that money. For years we struggled. When Ruby was a baby, I worked days and Merle worked nights, because we couldn't afford a sitter. But employment around here was scarce during the nineties. They call it the Rust Belt: there used to be loads of steel factories along this coastline, but they all closed down. We spent a good bit of Ruby's childhood on welfare. When Merle had his accident, I actually agreed with Julia that he should claim. It would have solved so many problems for us. But, like I said, she got to him. I suppose I could have tried for palimony, but I was too angry when he left, and I wanted to prove to him that the money didn't matter to me. Has Colm Barratt said anything about how Merle died?'

'Erm . . . ' Nell wondered how much to say. Colm was already angry with her, so she did not want to say the wrong thing. 'I don't think they're suspicious about it, because Merle hadn't been right since his accident.'

'That's just not true,' said Barbara. 'He was doing fine, apart from the problems with his hands. Look . . . '

She got up from the table and went to a long sideboard that stood in front of the window, picking up a picture in a frame. 'This was taken six months after his accident, when we spent a day on the beach.'

The picture showed a very different Merle, standing with Ruby and Barbara in front of an ice cream truck. He carried more weight on his body and around his face, and had a lot more hair. The sun had caught his nose, giving him a very healthy look. True, his hands were ravaged-looking, but if they had been hidden, no one would have guessed what he had gone through.

'Only his hands were damaged,' said Ruby. 'The rest of him was fine. But I saw him about a year after he married Julia and he'd changed completely. He was like a ghost.'

'Look,' said Nell, choosing her words carefully, 'I know it's hard when you lose someone you love. You look around for people to blame, and . . . '

'She killed him,' said Barbara emphatically. 'She killed her other husbands and she killed him. I know it in my heart.'

'I'm not . . . I don't know what I can

do for you,' said Nell. 'I'm not with the police.'

'No, but everyone says you're close to Chief Barratt,' said Ruby. 'You could talk to him and make him look at this as a murder.'

'I'm afraid he won't listen to anything I say,' Nell said. 'He's annoyed with me for investigating Julia as it is. He says that the police look into these things and that the results of the autopsy will . . . ' Nell stopped. She had said too much.

'Will what?' said Barbara, her brow furrowing.

'Will probably prove that Merle died from natural causes.'

'Oh . . . ' Barbara and Ruby both looked disappointed.

'I know how much you want to believe Julia killed him, but I don't think that's what happened.'

'What about all her other husbands?' asked Ruby.

'I don't know. Maybe she's just been very unlucky. Maybe she's drawn to men who are already sick, for whatever reason. I have a friend at the library where I work who always ends up caring for her boyfriends. It's as if she picks them sick and needy, in the same way that some women will always pick an abusive partner.'

'Julia is hardly Florence Nightingale,' said Barbara. 'She only pretended to be long enough for Merle to fall for her. I heard that she treated him terribly after they married.'

'Who knows what goes on in a marriage?' asked Nell, wondering where Barbara and Ruby got all their information about what happened on Barratt Island. 'I really should be going. I promised to call in at the hospital to see Wendy this afternoon.'

'We'd heard she'd had an accident,' said Barbara. 'Poor Wendy.'

'How come you know everyone on the island?' asked Nell. 'It's not as if you live close to them.'

'For a while last year I worked at the plant nursery over there,' said Barbara.

'It's a friendly place and I got to know everyone. That's how I know so much about Merle and Julia's marriage. She hated me working there but there was nothing she could do about it. In the end, I left of my own accord. It made for a long day by the time I took the ferry home.'

Nell said her goodbyes and got a taxi back to the hospital. No matter how much Barbara and Ruby wanted Julia blamed for Merle's death, Nell had to concede that it was probably not going to happen. No one had ever asked how one woman could be widowed so many times, but if Julia moved from place to place, people may not connect her with those men. Either she was innocent or she had covered her tracks very well. Not just with Merle but with her other husbands.

Almost as if thinking of her had conjured her up, when Nell reached Wendy's hotel room, she saw Julia standing over the bed, whispering frantically. 'Wake up and tell me,' she was saying. 'What did you tell Colm? What did you find out? I need to know. Tell me.'

'Ahem.' Nell coughed. Julia spun around, her eyes wide and startled.

'Nell, do you have to creep up like that?' she asked, with a small smile, quickly recovering.

'I'm sorry. I'd only just arrived. I mean . . . ' Nell wondered if she should let Julia know what she had heard, or whether to just leave it. As she saw it, either bringing it out into the open or keeping it secret left her at a disadvantage, as both might make Julia do something to silence her. 'What did you need to know from Wendy?' There, she had said it. At least here in the hospital Julia could not harm her, but she would have to be very careful.

'Yes, perhaps you might know, with you and Colm being . . . close.' Julia's lips pursed.

'I'm not aware of Wendy having told Colm anything,' said Nell. 'Honestly.'

'I just need to know,' said Julia.

'Because people are talking . . . they always talk . . . and I want to know what Wendy might have said. She hates me. She always has.'

'I'm sure that's not true. And if it is, why are you even here, Julia?'

'I'm trying to be neighbourly. Not that anyone on Barratt Island has ever been neighbourly to me. I'm the hired help's daughter, you know. My mother used to clean for the Barratts.'

'There's nothing wrong with that,' said Nell, gently. 'My mum worked as a cleaner too. It's how she paid for me to go to university.'

'I was never academic enough for that,' said Julia. She sat down in a chair next to Wendy's bed. 'My mother always said I had expensive tastes for a girl who couldn't even get a good grade in maths. But it's hard, you know, to see the Barratts get everything so easily, and then to have to work all the hours God sends for less than half of what they have.'

'But they all work, don't they? Colm

and his brothers? And Patty; I gather she's a lecturer at the college on the mainland.'

'They don't have to work. They choose to. There's a difference. And they still don't have to get their hands dirty like my mother did. Like I was expected to. Why shouldn't I have the good things in life, and as easily as they do?'

'Because . . . oh, I don't know,' said Nell, going to look out of the window. 'Because even if you have everything in life, it doesn't necessarily mean your life is easy. Colm lost his wife at a very young age. That has to hurt, and no amount of money can take that away. If you don't mind me saying, you and Merle were well-off after his settlement, but you weren't happy.'

'We were!' Julia protested. 'We were, until recently, when his health started to fail again. I just didn't know what to do with him. He was so unhappy.'

Nell turned to look at her, trying to work this woman out. Part of Nell wanted to shake her and tell her to get a grip. Millions — no, billions — of people had to work for a living so they could keep a roof over their heads and food on the table, let alone all the luxuries of modern living. None of them expected it to come easy.

On the other hand, she could almost see Julia as a child: growing up on the edges of wealth, seeing the Barratt children get everything they wanted and living what she saw as a charmed life. That could make a person feel bitter. But there was still the fact that when Julia had money she was no happier. She was one of those people who would never truly be satisfied, because there would always be someone with more than her. Better clothes or better furniture, or someone with a better-looking husband, like Mary Barratt with Colm. There was a sickness in Julia's heart that no amount of money could cure. Could that sickness lead her to murder? Or had she just been very unlucky in her choice of husbands?

Nell's mum always used to joke about wishing she had married 'a rich old man with a bad cough'. Maybe Julia had done just that, either wittingly or unwittingly.

Nell wondered if she should tell Colm about Julia pressing the unconscious Wendy for answers, but decided against it. He would only think she was being delusional again, and she could not bear the thought of him looking at her the way he had when she had first admitted to thinking Julia was a murderer.

'I'm sorry you're unhappy,' she said to Julia now. 'Truly I am. I hope you find the peace you seek, Julia. But I don't think you're going to find it by marrying a rich man.' She turned back to the window.

'Is that your way of warning me off Colm?' asked Julia, raising an eyebrow.

'Colm is free to choose whomever he wants,' said Nell, with a sad sigh. 'He doesn't belong to me, nor I to him.'

There was a moment's awkward

silence that was almost palpable. She turned around to see Colm standing at the door, looking straight at her, his face an inscrutable mask.

'I'd better go,' she said, with as much dignity as she could muster. 'I'm sure Wendy needs her rest.'

Wendy had little to say on the subject, still being unconscious, but Nell still felt bad about the way the conversation had turned. The poor woman was lying there stricken, whilst she and Julia had got into a spat about money and men.

Still, as Nell left — brushing past Colm, who was half-blocking the door — she wondered what Julia had been trying to find out from Wendy . . . and whether her friend would be safe if Nell did not speak up and tell someone about it.

* * *

The weeks rolled on, until it was late August and Nell only had a month left of her holiday. At times she had silently screamed in frustration at being stuck on Barratt Island. Not literally stuck. She could go to the mainland whenever she wanted, but she could not go home, which was what she desperately wanted to do.

In her own village, which was on the edge of a large conurbation, she could go months, even years, without seeing someone. On Barratt Island, she could barely go a day without seeing Colm in the distance. Every sighting of him was like a dagger, and she imagined her heart as a pin cushion, pierced dozens of times over.

It occurred to her that anywhere could be a heaven or hell, depending on your outlook. Barratt Island had seemed like heaven, and still had the capacity to be that. But with Colm not talking to her, Wendy in the hospital and Julia giving her icy glares every time she stepped out the front door, the island was becoming a hell on earth.

'How do you do that?' she asked her reflection late one night. 'How do you manage to mess up everything? You can't leave here yet, and even when you can, you have to go home and face the neighbours who think you're a joke.'

The place of peace had become a prison to her.

She spent as much time as possible on the mainland, only returning to the island to sleep at nights. Anything to avoid Colm. He was busy with a case involving a burglary of one of the more expensive properties on the island. Nell wondered if the results of Merle's autopsy had come back yet, but even if she had someone to ask about it, she dared not.

A lot of the time, she ate at Vinnie's, becoming a regular there. Vinnie was always warm and welcoming. A couple of times she had dinner with Ruby and Barbara Silkwood, but those times were strained. It seemed to Nell that they only wanted to know what Colm might have told her and as soon as they realised he was not speaking to Nell at all, the invitations to dinner subsided.

Then she came back to Canopache one night to find a message on the answerphone.

'Ms Palmer, this is Detective Inspector Underwood of the Derbyshire Constabulary. It is imperative that I speak with you as soon as possible.'

* * *

Colm drove past Canopache late in the evening, wondering why everything was in darkness. He knew that Nell had been spending a lot of time away from the island, but he also knew that she always returned on the last ferry. That had come back an hour ago, and he had been looking out for her. He wanted to talk to her and to clear the air. Whatever happened, he did not want her to end her vacation on a sour note.

She may well be delusional, but she was also charming and kind and gorgeous. He had not felt this way about a woman since his wife Mary had died, and there had been a time he thought he never would again.

He stopped his pick-up truck and knocked on the door. There was no answer. Maybe she was avoiding him still, but he was worried about her. For a while he had fought the feeling that something was happening on Barratt Island. His prejudice against Nell, because of what Patty had told him, had stifled his normal police instincts. It was time for him to stop denying the truth and start being a police officer again. Whether Julia had killed her husband he did not know, but when he looked back over the past few weeks of Merle Silkwood's life, he could see that things were not quite right. He made a mental note to contact the pathologist and hurry along the test results.

Determined that something awful must have happened to Nell, he used his spare key to unlock the door to Canopache, and went inside.

'Nell?' he called, but to no avail. The

whole house was in darkness. It occurred to him that if she had just gone down to the marina for a meal, she would be annoyed to find him lurking around the house. But she had not just gone out for a meal. He could sense that by the feel of the house. It had the same atmosphere as it had the day before Nell arrived; a house that had been closed up and left empty.

To satisfy his curiosity, he went upstairs to the main bedroom. The bed had been made up with clean linen, and the closet that had been set aside for Nell's use was open. Colm went to open it wider and saw that it was empty. No clothes. No suitcases. He checked the ensuite and saw that all the toiletries had gone too. No handbags, no passports. Nothing to show that she had ever been there.

Sitting on the bed, Colm put his head in his hands. Nell had left, and she had not even said goodbye.

It was an hour later, after driving around the island looking for her, thinking that she might have just moved into a hotel, that he finally gave up and went home, having learned that Nell had left on the very last ferry for the mainland.

The hall telephone was ringing as he unlocked the door.

'Nell?' he said, when he answered, praying that she had phoned to say goodbye.

'No, honey, it's me, Patty. But I'm calling about Nell. Did she get the message from the British police?'

'What message?' asked Colm. 'She's gone, Patty. Disappeared, and she didn't even say goodbye.'

There was a momentary silence, and Colm knew his big sister well enough to know that she was considering the implications of what he had just said. She knew him well enough to realise that Nell's absence mattered to him. 'She had to come back to England, honey,' said Patty, gently. 'So I guess she's on her way back.'

'Why? Is she in trouble with the

police? Tell me, Patty, and I'll do all I can to help her. I have an old friend who works in Scotland Yard, and . . . '

Patty laughed. 'She's not in trouble. Far from it. Oh Colm, you've no idea what has been going on here. Police have been digging up the next door neighbour's garden. Mr Kemp? The guy I told you about? It's all over the local news, though I guess it hasn't reached the States yet.'

'What? What's happened?'

'That 'nice' Mr Kemp turns out not to be have been so nice after all,' said Patty. 'Colm, Nell was right all along. Well, almost right. It wasn't his wife that he murdered. It was his lover, and he buried her in the garden!'

10

It was two days before Nell finally got home. She had to stop over in New York, and then stop again near Heathrow when she arrived too late to travel north. To say she was exhausted the next morning was an understatement; but, once back in Derbyshire, she took a taxi straight to the local police station.

'Thank you for coming back so quickly, Ms Palmer,' said DI Underwood. 'And can I start by apologising, on behalf of the Derbyshire Constabulary, for the way you've been treated in the past?'

'It didn't help that I thought it was Mrs Kemp and that she turned up alive and well,' said Nell with a small smile. She still burned with the humiliation of the way she had been treated previously, but now was not the time for recriminations. A woman really was dead, and Nell was too noble a person to find pleasure in being proved right

'That's not your fault either,' said DI Underwood. 'The victim looked very much like Mrs Kemp. In fact, I'd go so far as to say that Mr Kemp has a type. She wasn't his only lover, though thankfully the others are still alive. A few came forward after you left for America, to testify to the fact that he could be violent. Then this lady was declared missing, and the last person she was seen with was Kemp, which gave us an excuse to search his house. All we need now from you is a new statement to tell us what you saw on the night he killed her.'

Nell nodded. It was hours before she was finished at the station, and she intended to book into a hotel. When she got to the foyer of the police station, a woman was waiting for her. She was about forty-five years old, willowy and beautiful, but there was something familiar about her eyes.

'Hi, Nell, I'm Patty. DI Underwood let me know you were back. I thought I'd come to take you home.'

'Hello, Patty. I'm so glad to meet you at last! But really, I can book into a hotel. The house is still yours for another few weeks.'

'Nonsense! It's your home, and the last thing you want after such a long journey is the expense and discomfort of another hotel.'

Patty bundled Nell into a taxi, and took her home, where the aroma of beef stew filled the cottage. For the next hour, Patty refused to let Nell do anything other than eat the delicious stew and drink Prosecco. Then she made sure Nell went to bed, but thankfully fell short of tucking her in.

'Thank you, Patty,' said Nell, sinking into her own bed and feeling exhaustion wash over her.

'I promised Colm I'd take care of you,' said Patty as she put a cup of tea next to the bed. 'Anyway, I feel guilty, because . . . well . . . I told Colm about what happened with Kemp the first time.'

'It wasn't a huge secret,' said Nell. 'So I don't blame you. Not at all. Besides, I didn't help by deciding that Julia Silkwood murdered her husband . . . '

'That wouldn't have surprised me at all,' said Patty, in no-nonsense tones.

'Really?'

'Yes. Colm has a very romantic view of women. That's because Mary was such an angel. He finds it hard to believe any of them could do anything bad. But Julia has always been difficult. I don't say it does make her a murderer; I can just understand why you thought so.'

'Well, it's over now,' said Nell. She turned into her pillow, and was glad that Patty left the bedroom. The enormity of everything that had happened suddenly hit her. She felt a mixture of relief and exhaustion, but also grief for what might have been with Colm. She cried herself to sleep.

The following morning, she awoke to the aroma of bacon and fresh coffee. Rubbing her eyes, she made her way downstairs to the kitchen. Her kitchen. The thought made her emotional again. She had missed her little house, but in an odd way she missed Canopache and Barratt Island too. Strange, that only a couple of days before, she had seen it as a prison. She felt much like a prisoner who had been let out on lease and did not know what to do with her newfound freedom.

'Good morning,' said Patty, pouring a cup of coffee and pointing to the breakfast bar. 'Now you sit and eat, and drink.

'It's ten o'clock,' said Nell, looking at the wall clock. 'I never sleep this late.' She sat on the stool and took a slice of toast out of the stand, spreading it with thick, creamy butter.

'Well, you needed it, honey. Colm called earlier, but I told him there was no way I was waking you. But he has good news. Wendy has woken up.'

'Oh I'm so relieved,' said Nell. For some reason she started to cry again. Patty crossed the kitchen and put her arms around her.

'Don't cry, honey. Colm is going to sort everything out. Now, you try and eat. You need your strength.'

★ ★ ★

Colm gave Wendy's husband time to visit before going in to question her.

'She's a little bit out of it,' said Ted, 'But she wants to talk to you.'

'Did she say how she came to be injured?' asked Colm.

Ted shrugged. 'She says it was just the storm. She was in the den when the roof caved in.'

'Okay,' said Colm, dismissing one line of thought. It was a relief, as he did not like the idea of someone harming Wendy in order to silence her.

'Colm,' said Wendy, when he went to sit at her bedside. Her voice was a little croaky.

'Hi, Wendy. We're all delighted that you're awake. The guys at the station send their love. Are you okay to answer questions?'

'I'll do my best. I know there was something I wanted to tell you.'

'Can you remember?'

'I think so. I mean, some things are a bit hazy, but I remember what I needed to tell you. I was doing the stock-taking for old man Wharton at the nursery, and there was a discrepancy. Several packs of pesticide were unaccounted for. I asked Mr Wharton if he'd taken them out of stock to use in the nursery, but he was sure he hadn't. So we put it down to someone shoplifting. But that doesn't happen here on Barratt Island.'

'Well, the odd kid tries their luck, but no, we don't get a lot of it,' Colm agreed. 'And I can't see kids taking pesticide. Ice creams out of the cooler maybe, or even glue if they're into sniffing it. But pesticide seems an odd choice for a shoplifter unless they have something planned.'

'And I got to thinking about Merle,' said Wendy, 'and how he was looking worse as the weeks wore on, and . . . Oh Colm, it's a dreadful thing to think, with Julia being our friend, but . . . '

'You're not the only one to think so,' said Colm. 'But it would be a big risk for Julia to shoplift. She could just buy pesticide and say she's using it in the garden.'

'I wish I could remember everything. Old man Wharton should know.'

'I'll go talk to him. Don't you worry about it now. Just concentrate on getting better. Meanwhile, I've got one of the guys waiting outside. If there's any trouble, he'll step in.'

Colm left Wendy, and went to a different part of the hospital to find the pathologist. Verity Owen was a good-looking girl in her early thirties. But she was also extremely harassed.

'Any news on my autopsy?' Colm asked her. 'It's been a while now, Verity.'

'Sorry, Chief Barratt,' said Verity.

'But we've had people off sick, and I was away on vacation. Then we had that big pile-up on the highway. You did say it wasn't urgent.'

'Things might have changed,' said Colm, embarrassed by his earlier inadequacy. He should have taken Nell more seriously. If she was right about Mr Kemp being a killer, even if she had got the details wrong, then she could be right about Julia. 'I've since had reason to believe that there was foul play involved.' He tried not to think too much of Nell. It hurt to imagine her so many thousands of miles away from him, and to think that maybe he drove her away. True, the British police had wanted her back, but they would not have expected her to return quite so quickly. He could not fight the feeling she had used it as an excuse to leave early.

'Okay, give me an hour,' said Verity, 'and I'll have some answers for you.'

'I have to get back to the island, so

call me,' said Colm. 'You know how to reach me.'

He took the ferry back, and picked up his car from the marina before driving up to Julia's. On the way, he called on his radio for a woman officer to be present.

Coincidentally, Julia was working in her garden when he arrived. With fall around the corner, the first leaves had started to flutter from the trees, and she was raking them up. She looked up and smiled when she saw Colm pull up. As he did, his phone rang. It was Verity, with the information he needed. He made a few more phone calls whilst he waited.

Meryl Farmer, the only woman police officer on Barratt Island, arrived a couple of minutes later. She was a pretty black woman with a hundred-watt smile and a kind word for those who needed it, but anyone who thought she was a pushover soon learned otherwise.

Colm got out of his car, and waited

until Meryl had got out of hers. 'Julia
. . . Ms Silkwood . . . could we have a
word with you, please?'

'That sounds very formal, Colm,'
said Julia. She looked around as if
afraid they might be seen. There was no
one on the road or in the immediate
vicinity, but the beach, a hundred yards
away, was packed with holidaymakers.
'You'd better come inside.'

Colm waited until they were all
seated in Julia's pristine living room.
'Julia, I need to ask you a few questions.
We can do it here or down at the
station. It's up to you.'

'Oh . . . ' Julia smiled disarmingly.
'Do I need a lawyer?'

'I don't know. Do you?' Colm gave
her a searching look.

'No, of course not, Colm. I'm not
under arrest, am I? We're all friends,
aren't we?'

'You're not under arrest yet,' said
Colm. 'But the fact is, Julia, that
Merle's autopsy results have just come
back, and it seems he was poisoned.'

'What?' Julia looked genuinely surprised, but Colm was beginning to wonder if she was just a very good actress.

'There were traces of pesticide in his blood. The same pesticide that went missing from the plant nursery not long ago. Do you know anything about that?'

'No. Certainly not.'

'You and Merle were having problems,' Colm said. It was a statement rather than a question.

'Yes, we were having problems. I believed Merle was seeing someone else. They kept sending him cards. And chocolates.'

'What chocolates?'

'Boxes of them. The handmade kind stores charge a fortune for. I told him they were bad for him.'

'Who sent them?'

'I don't know. That's the idea of a secret admirer, I suppose. They remain a secret. But I think Merle knew who it was. He just wasn't saying.'

'Do you have any of these chocolates in the house?'

Julia shook her head. 'No, I threw them all out after he died.'

'And you didn't eat any?' said Meryl.

'Of course not. I have to watch my figure. Besides, if they were sent by his lover, I didn't want anything to do with them. I know what you're all thinking, I know what that Nell Palmer was thinking — but I did not murder my husband, and I will sue anyone who says otherwise!'

'There's nothing you can tell us to shed light on this?' said Colm.

'Nothing.'

'We're going to need you to come down to the station and make a statement,' said Colm. 'Will you do that?'

'I suppose I must.'

'Meryl, can you take her in?' asked Colm. 'I need to make some calls. I'd also like to get the CSI team in here. Is that okay with you, Julia?'

'I . . . yes, if you want to. I've nothing

to hide, Colm, and I must say I'm disappointed in you. I thought we were friends.'

'Friends or not, I have to do my job, Julia.' Inwardly, he winced at his own words. It was a pity he had not thought of that weeks ago. 'Are you sure you have nothing left of the chocolates you say that Merle received? No packaging with postal markings?'

'I just threw it in the bin. You can hardly blame me. Why should I keep the mementos of his secret admirer around?'

Colm searched her face, but realised he wouldn't get anything else from her. 'And you never ate any of the chocolates?'

'I told you. No.'

'There's something else. Nell Palmer said she was sick after you made her a chocolate cake. Is there any reason that might have happened?'

Julia scoffed. 'Are you suggesting I poisoned her? I barely knew the woman when I made it. That's what you get for being neighbourly. Of course, I never liked her, and everyone knows the woman is delusional. Why on earth would I poison her?'

'I don't know why anyone would poison Nell, or Merle for that matter. That's what I'm trying to work out.'

Meryl took Julia back to the station, and the CSI team arrived to sweep the house. They worked quietly and thoroughly and without trying to form any conclusions of their own, unlike in the television shows. Their search yielded nothing. They even checked the trash, in the hopes of finding the boxes or packaging, but to no avail. Either Julia had been careful to clear out any evidence, or there was no evidence to find.

Meanwhile, Colm made calls all over the country to find out about Julia's previous husbands.

'She certainly buried a lot of husbands,' Colm told his sister in a telephone call later that night. He was back at home, and trying to chill out, but he could not settle.

'So Nell was right?' said Patty.

'I don't know.' Colm rubbed his eyes with his hands. 'We're having the bodies exhumed. And we're trying to find out what happened at the nursery.'

He heard his sister speak to someone in the background, and realised it was Nell. He heard her ask, 'Could I speak to him? It's important, Patty.'

'Nell would like to speak to you,' said Patty.

'Sure. Put her on,' said Colm. His heart began to beat a little faster.

'Hello, Colm . . . how are you?' Her voice was reserved but not cold. He was sure it trembled a little, but that might have been the telephone line.

'Worn out at the moment.'

'I'm sorry.'

'No,' he said. 'It's not your fault.'

'It's just that Patty told me that the pesticide that killed Merle probably came from the local plant nursery.'

'That's right.'

'Well . . . it might not be relevant, but

I'm sure that Barbara Silkwood told me that she worked there for a while. Unless it was a different plant nursery on Barratt Island.'

Colm sat up straight. 'No, there's only the one. Old man Wharton's. When was this?'

'I don't know. She only said that it was for a short while, and that she stopped because it was a long day for her after taking the ferry back to the mainland.'

'Well, thanks, Nell. I'll look into it.'

'I'm glad to have helped. I mean, I'm sure there's nothing to it, but . . . '

'All information is helpful. Look, I owe you an apology for doubting you.'

'It doesn't matter,' said Nell, her usually soft voice sounding brittle. 'Forget it. I hope you find Merle's killer, whoever it is. He seemed to be a nice man.'

'Nell . . . ' Colm started to say, but she had already handed the phone back to Patty. After speaking to his sister for a while about the family and other local gossip, he put the phone down and went to bed.

He could not sleep. He kept seeing Nell as she had been on the day they made love. It had been one of the happiest days of his life, and he had blown it to the point of putting the Atlantic Ocean between them.

★   ★   ★

Across that ocean, albeit several hours later, Nell also tried to sleep, but hearing Colm's voice had unnerved her. She too kept remembering the day they made love. Colm had shown her a passion she had never experienced. But his harsh words afterwards had hurt her deeply, especially in light of her learning the truth about Mr Kemp. How could they ever go back to the warmth they had shared? Especially with so many thousands of miles between them.

She would never return to America, and she doubted he would come to her.

She had fallen in love with him, and knew that she would never love anyone as she had loved him. She had never loved anyone in that way. Not even Rick, who had just been the equivalent of a comfort blanket.

No wonder her ex-husband found solace with another woman, she thought. She had never really shown him the love and affection he needed. That he had never shown her affection, or even commitment, did not occur to her in the self-pitying state in which she now found herself. She wondered, if Julia were cleared of wrongdoing, whether Colm would find solace with her.

11

Colm turned his police car into the main road leading to Barren Island, the area where Ruby and Barbara Silkwood lived. Nell's information had led to more discoveries, and it was time to face Barbara with the truth. How much her daughter knew, he could not have said.

Another unmarked police car was parked across the road from the single-storey house, and the occupant waved to him and got out. It was Meryl Farmer. They walked up to the house together.

'Colm, what a lovely surprise,' said Barbara when she answered the door. 'It's been a while.'

'Yeah, it has. Where is Ruby?'

'She's at college.'

'Good, then we can have a quiet chat. You know Meryl Farmer, I take it?' He gestured to his colleague, who had just got out of the other car. Meryl had been watching the house all morning.

'This is all very official,' said Barbara, bustling them into the house. He had to admit she was more welcoming than Julia had been under the same circumstances. 'Can I make you coffee? Tea? What about a cold beer, Colm? It's a hot day. Do you think it will bring more tourists? I hope so, because I really need a job.'

'That's what we've come to talk to you about,' said Colm, stepping into Barbara's front room. Compared to Julia's spotless house, Barbara's was 'lived in', but still clean.

'You're going to offer me a job?' said Barbara, smiling. But there was something behind her eyes. Some sort of reserve.

'I'm afraid not. We wanted to talk to you about the time you worked at Old Man Wharton's. The plant nursery. That was about three months ago, wasn't it?'

'Oh, yes.'

'Wendy — you know Wendy?'

'Yes, I do.'

'She's been helping Wharton stock-take, and found there were discrepancies regarding the loss of some pesticides. We've been looking through the records, and they went missing around the time you were there.'

'What are you saying, Colm? That I stole pesticide? Have you seen my garden? I keep it as neat as I can, but wildlife flourishes there quite happily. Ruby likes it that way. Do you know there's a thing about the colour of snails meaning changes in the climate? She's studying it all in college.'

'No, I didn't know that. Can you account for why the pesticide went missing? Someone had been sending Merle chocolates. Now, we have no proof, because all the chocolates are gone, but we think that's how he was poisoned. But we *do* know that the same pesticide that went missing from Old Man Wharton's was in Merle's bloodstream. So you're looking at a murder charge, Barbara.'

'Oh.' Barbara put her hands to her mouth. She slumped down in a chair. 'I didn't kill him. Julia did. It was Julia. She's behind this . . . Oh, it wasn't even my idea,' she said, bursting into tears.

'What wasn't your idea?' asked Colm.

'He said it was the only way to be free of her and keep the money.'

'What was?' Colm frowned. 'You'd better tell me everything, Barbara.' He pulled out a chair from the dining table, and spun it around, straddling it like a marshal in an old western.

'When I started working at the plant nursery, Merle came in a few times, and we got talking. He said he regretted leaving me and Ruby and that he wished we could be a family again. We met up once or twice — he'd come over the mainland to see us. I don't think Julia ever guessed. We started an affair. I asked him to leave her, but he said that if he did, she would want half of his settlement. So he came up with this idea. We found out that she'd had lots of husbands, and it seemed like she might have killed them. Merle decided that if she was accused of trying to kill him too, she wouldn't be able to have the money. At first I told him it was ridiculous, but he insisted on going along with it, and that I help him. I knew that if I left him to his own devices he'd make a mess of it all. So I got him the pesticide, and he did the rest. Finding the chocolates and telling Julia they'd been sent to him. He figured he'd deny that the moment she was arrested. Only . . . only he overdid it, I think. He even poisoned that English lady, Nell.'

'How?'

'He said that Julia had made Nell a chocolate cake, and whilst Julia wasn't looking, he tipped some pesticide in. Not enough to kill her. Just enough so she would be sick and then testify later that Julia had sent her a poisoned cake. Merle knew that Julia liked you, you see, and that Nell was just the sort of lady to attract you, so he could make out that Julia was getting rid of the opposition. But, like I said, when he poisoned his own food he overdid it, and it killed him anyway. But she did kill her other husbands. She did!'

'We'll find out soon enough if that is true. But right now, Barbara, I'm arresting you for supplying lethal poison. Whether you'll be charged with manslaughter is up to the District Attorney.' He read her the Miranda warning as Meryl Farmer put her into cuffs.

'Ruby doesn't know any of this,' said Barbara. 'She's completely innocent. She really believes Julia killed her father.'

★   ★   ★

As Colm was reading Barbara her rights, Nell was putting her suitcases down in the hallway of Canopache. 'Are you sure I should go back there?' she had asked Patty as they waved goodbye at Heathrow Airport.

'Yes, of course. You need the break, and the British police won't need you for a trial now that Mr Kemp has committed suicide. You're needed there.'

'I feel like Jessica Fletcher,' Nell had said, grimacing. 'Always turning up where there's murder and mayhem. Are you sure Colm won't throw me into prison?'

'I think he's probably got much nicer plans for you than that.'

Over the days that Nell had been back in Britain, Patty had teased the truth about Nell and Colm out of her. Nell had fallen short of describing the day of stormy passion, but Patty was an insightful woman and had been able to fill in the blanks.

'You should go back to America,' she had insisted. 'You still have nearly a month left in the house.'

When Nell had finally admitted she could not afford the air fare, Patty had gone online and booked the flights herself. 'You can pay me back later,' she said.

So, once again, Nell was at Canopache. She had to admit, as the ferry crossed the channel between the mainland and the island, that it was like coming home. At least she might be able to resolve things with Colm so that they could part as friends.

She looked over the road and saw that all Julia's curtains were drawn. She knew that Julia had been questioned and then released, but whilst she had realised Barbara was involved somehow, she did not yet know the full details — or how Merle had, allegedly, planned everything to discredit Julia.

Nell went to the kitchen to make a much-needed cup of tea — the Yorkshire teabags that Colm had bought her were still in the cupboard, causing a pang of emotion to sear through her — and then stood drinking it, looking out the window. She needed to speak to Julia too, to apologise and clear the air. She thought about the chocolate cake in the freezer and wondered if she should try it again. It would take a while to defrost, but maybe she could put a slice in the microwave.

She took the cake out and hacked off a slice, putting it in the microwave to defrost for five minutes.

As she was waiting dusk began to fall, and she saw someone walking up the road towards Julia's. Whoever it was wore a hoody covering their head, and unisex clothes, so it was hard to tell if it was a slender man or a woman. The fine hairs on the back of Nell's neck stood on end as the figure turned into Julia's gate. She saw a glint of something as the setting sun caught it, and realised it was a knife.

Dropping her cup with a clatter on the parquet flooring, Nell flung open the French doors and ran across the garden. 'Stop!' she called, as the figure reached Julia's front door and rang the bell. 'Stop!'

The figure turned, and Nell immedi-ately recognised the black eyeliner and a flash of red hair. 'Ruby . . . '

At that moment, Julia's door opened and the woman herself stood there. 'What is it? What do you want?' Nell heard her say.

'Julia, shut the door, quickly!'

But before that happened, Ruby flung herself at Julia, knocking her to the ground. There was a struggle for the knife, and Nell ran hell for leather up the steps to try to stop the worst from happening.

'Ruby, this is not the right way,' she cried, reaching over Ruby's back and struggling for the knife. Ruby pulled her elbow back sharply into Nell's ribs, knocking the wind out of her. Nell fell to her knees.

'She killed my father,' said Ruby, sobbing, but Nell's intervention seemed to have halted her attack on Julia, who managed to crawl further into the hallway, out of harm's way. At least for that moment.

'No . . . no, she didn't,' gasped Nell. 'Your mum . . . the pesticide . . . the nursery,' she stammered breathlessly, unable to make sense of it herself. 'Oh Ruby, I'm so sorry.'

'My mom didn't kill my dad. She loved him.'

'I don't know exactly what happened, but Julia didn't murder your dad. Wait to speak to Colm. He'll tell you everything. But even if Julia had killed your dad, you don't want to do this. Merle wouldn't want you to do this. It will ruin your life, and you're so young. You have so much potential. Don't throw it all away. If you walk away now, I'm sure Julia won't press charges. Right, Julia?' Nell was vaguely aware of a car coming up the road. She prayed that it was someone who could help them with this situation and that they would not just drive past.

'I . . . ' Julia pursed her lips, and looked as if she might protest. 'Yeah, right. We'll forget it.'

'What about her other husbands? What about any men she marries in the future? She killed them all. We know she did, me and mom.'

'I didn't kill them,' said Julia, her mouth turning up at the corners in a wry and rather ugly smile. 'I just got good at picking . . . ' She paused.

'Old men with bad coughs,' said Nell, distastefully.

'Yeah, something like that. And why shouldn't I? Why shouldn't I have the same sort of life as the Barratts? Why shouldn't I have Colm Barratt? Though I guess now you're back, I can forget that.'

'She killed them and I'd be doing the world a favour,' said Ruby, her anger rising again.

'No!' Julia and Nell cried.

'Ruby . . . ' a female voice said from behind them. 'Put the knife away, baby.'

'Mom . . . ' Ruby stood up unsteadily and faced her mother with tears in her eyes. 'Mom?'

Barbara stood there, flanked by Colm and Meryl Farmer. 'I'm sorry, baby. Your dad . . . I'd have done anything for him, including freeing him from her, but she didn't kill him, no matter how much we'd like to believe it. He killed himself in the end. Not intentionally, but he played with fire and got burned. Now I need you to be a brave girl for me.'

'Mommy?' Ruby dropped the knife and threw herself at her mother, sobbing.

Meryl lead Barbara back to the police car, closely followed by Ruby. Colm turned to look at Nell and simply said, 'You're back.'

'Yep. Looks like it.'

'Good. Good . . .'

Because she did not know what else to say to him, Nell spoke to Julia instead. 'Julia, I'm really sorry. It's my fault you were suspected.'

'Not entirely,' Colm interjected.

'I was so silly over that chocolate cake,' Nell continued. 'I still have it. Maybe we could get together for coffee and cake and talk things over. I've just defrosted some.'

'You still have the cake?' Colm

interrupted again, before Julia could answer.

'Yes, it's in the microwave.'

Colm laughed. 'Then I'm going to have to take it as evidence. Julia didn't try to poison you, Nell. But Merle did. According to Barbara, he spiked the cake with pesticide.'

'Oh . . . ' Bile rose in Nell's throat and her knees turned to jelly. 'Oh, God . . . '

12

'Are you all right?' Colm faced Nell across the kitchen counter. It was the morning after all the excitement with Ruby and Julia.

'I'm fine, really. I just can't quite believe I saved Julia's life.' She laughed. 'Goodness what does that comment say about me?'

'She doesn't make it easy for people to like her.'

'Is Ruby okay? That poor girl has been through so much. First losing her dad and now she's going to lose her mum.'

'She's fine. We've persuaded Julia not to press charges. It wasn't easy, but we suggested that if it went to court, then Julia's previous marriages would come under scrutiny.'

'She says she just got good at picking men who were going to die. Do you believe that?'

'Maybe. We've investigated all her other husbands and if she did kill them, she was very clever about it. There's nothing we can pin on her. So it seems she's going to walk away this time, but maybe it will make her more careful in the future.'

'Just be careful, Colm.'

'Careful? Me? Why?'

'I mean, if you and Julia get together. Not that she shouldn't have every reason to love you. But I'm not sure she'll ever be truly satisfied, and even a man as perfect as you will seem flawed to her after a while.'

'I'm glad you think I'm perfect.'

'Oh, well, you are. You're handsome, charming and kind.'

'Rich . . . '

'That doesn't matter. I mean, it shouldn't matter. Not to anyone. But that's the trouble, isn't it? You'll never know for sure.' She grinned wryly. 'It must be such a curse, having all that money.'

'I bear it well, I think.' He smiled back.

Nell laughed. 'I honestly don't know how you cope from day to day.'

'I'm not sure I do.'

'Oh, go on, poor little rich boy.'

'What I mean is that you can have all the money in the world and still feel like there's something missing in your life.'

'That's probably how Julia feels.'

'I'm not talking about Julia. It was never an issue, you know. Me and Julia. Whatever she might have thought, I would never have married her. She's too tightly-wound for me. My wife Mary was like a faerie princess, with her head in the clouds. Man, she could spin a yarn. I used to say to her that she should write children's books, but she saved all her stories for Kathleen.'

'I'm sorry I never got to meet your daughter.'

'Why are you talking in the past tense? You're still here. There's still time.'

'I have to go home,' said Nell. 'I only

came to tie up loose ends, I suppose. I just wanted us to part as friends.' She stretched her hand across the counter. 'We are friends, aren't we?'

Colm took a step back, his eyebrows knitting in the middle. 'I don't think I want to be your friend.'

'Oh. Well, I can't blame you for that under the circumstances.' Nell coloured up, then indignation set in. 'Hang on a minute, Colm. I was right. About Mr Kemp being a killer and about Merle being poisoned. Okay, I may have got the exact details wrong, but I knew something was wrong in both cases. How can you still be angry with me about that?'

'I'm not angry with you about that. I'm angry that after everything that's happened, you still insist on going home.'

'Well, what else can I do? I have a job and a home. I can't stay here forever.'

'Why not?'

'I think Patty might want her house back for a start.'

'There are other houses on Barratt Island.'

'Hmm, they're a bit out of my reach.'

'What about that shack in my back yard?'

Thinking he was joking, she said, 'That's a possibility. Does it have running water?'

'No. You'd have to use my shower and facilities.'

'Oh.'

'In fact, there's not even room for a bed. So you'd have to use one of my bedrooms.'

'Are you asking me to lodge with you?'

'No, you wonderful, hare-brained, woman, I'm asking you to marry me. And I mean now, this minute. Not in ten years' time, and if you think I'm visiting you twice a week for marital privileges, you've got another think coming. We're going to be a proper husband and wife. There will be lots of sex.'

'Oh.' Nell put her hand to her

mouth. 'Really.' She grinned. 'Starting when?'

'Oh no, you have to say you'll marry me first. I'm not easy, you know.'

'Actually you were really easy. A bit of a storm and a blackout, and you were anybody's.'

He walked around the counter and caught her by the waist. 'Not anybody's, Lady Nell. Just yours. I love you. I've loved you since the day you arrived. I even loved you when I thought you were a lunatic.'

'That's comforting.'

He gazed into her eyes. 'Don't you love me just a little bit?'

'No. Not a little bit.'

His face dropped. 'I see.'

'I love you more than anything in the world. I was afraid I'd never see you again. That's why I came back. I thought if I could just see you once, it would keep me going for a lifetime. Now I know I can't bear to leave. Oh Colm, darling, can we make it work, do you think? I don't want to get it all wrong again.'

He pulled her into his arms and answered her with a kiss.

Hours later, lying safely in his arms, Nell knew she had found her place of peace.

THE END

We do hope that you have enjoyed reading this large print book.

Did you know that all of our titles are available for purchase?

We publish a wide range of high quality large print books including:
Romances, Mysteries, Classics
General Fiction
Non Fiction and Westerns

Special interest titles available in large print are:
The Little Oxford Dictionary
Music Book, Song Book
Hymn Book, Service Book

Also available from us courtesy of Oxford University Press:
Young Readers' Dictionary
(large print edition)
Young Readers' Thesaurus
(large print edition)

For further information or a free brochure, please contact us at:
Ulverscroft Large Print Books Ltd.,
The Green, Bradgate Road, Anstey,
Leicester, LE7 7FU, England.
Tel: (00 44) **0116 236 4325**
Fax: (00 44) **0116 234 0205**

*Other titles in the
Linford Romance Library:*

ROMANCE IN THE AIR

Pat Posner

After ending a relationship she discovered was based on lies, Annie Layton has sworn off men. When her employers, Edmunds' Airways, tell her they're expanding, she eagerly agrees to help set up the sister company. Moving up north will get her away from her ex — and the Air Ministry official who's been playing havoc with her emotions. But Annie hadn't known exactly who she'd be working with . . . Will she find herself pitched headlong into further heartache?

ANGELA'S RETURN HOME

Margaret Mounsdon

It has been years since schoolteacher Angela Banks last saw Russ Stretton, but she remembers him only too well. She'd had a massive crush on him as a teenager, and now he was back in her life. But he's carrying considerable emotional baggage, including a five-year-old son, Mikey — not to mention a sophisticated French ex-wife, who seems intent on winning him back at all costs . . .